SAVAGE FOES

The officers and the expectant soldiers all about him saw the horseman close enough to make out what Maximus had already realized. The messenger, a high-ranking Roman officer, was strapped to his horse, headless.

Maximus watched the dead man ride toward them, his torso swaying grotesquely in the saddle, drenched in streams of blood. Maximus's face was a stone mask, showing nothing but steady concentration.

"I'll crucify them!" Quintus shouted.

Out of the same dense wood far across the no-man's-land, a German tribesman appeared in an animal-skin cloak. He raised the severed head of the Roman envoy by the hair in a bloody display of defiance. He screamed in visceral rage at the army spread out before him. The Roman troops stared back impassively.

The German chieftain swung back his arm and hurled the severed head toward them, bouncing and rolling in the mire.

"A people should know when they're conquered," Quintus rasped with loathing.

Maximus kept his eyes on the enraged tribesman. "Would you?"

GLADIATOR

Dewey Gram

BASED ON A
SCREENPLAY BY

David Franzoni

AND

John Logan

AND

William Nicholson

STORY BY

David Franzoni

AN ONYX BOOK

ONYX
Published by New American Library, a division of
Penguin Putnam Inc., 375 Hudson Street,
New York, New York 10014, U.S.A.
Penguin Books Ltd, 27 Wrights Lane,
London W8 5TZ, England
Penguin Books Australia Ltd, Ringwood,
Victoria, Australia
Penguin Books Canada Ltd, 10 Alcorn Avenue,
Toronto, Ontario, Canada M4V 3B2
Penguin Books (N.Z.) Ltd, 182–190 Wairau Road,
Auckland 10, New Zealand

Penguin Books Ltd, Registered Offices:
Harmondsworth, Middlesex, England

First published by Onyx, an imprint of New American Library,
a division of Penguin Putnam Inc.

First Printing, May 2000
10 9 8 7 6 5 4

 REGISTERED TRADEMARK—MARCA REGISTRADA

AT THE HEIGHT OF ITS POWER, THE VAST ROMAN EMPIRE STRETCHED FROM THE DESERTS OF AFRICA TO THE BORDERS OF NORTHERN ENGLAND.

OVER ONE QUARTER OF THE WORLD'S POPULATION LIVED AND DIED UNDER THE RULE OF THE CAESARS.

IN THE WINTER OF A.D. 180, EMPEROR MARCUS AURELIUS'S TWELVE-YEAR CAMPAIGN AGAINST BARBARIAN TRIBES IN GERMANIA WAS DRAWING TO AN END.

ONE FINAL STRONGHOLD STOOD IN THE WAY OF ROMAN VICTORY AND THE PROMISE OF PEACE THROUGHOUT THE EMPIRE.

ONE

The wheat was high and lush as he walked through the sun-warmed field, trailing a hand and letting the swollen grain spikes pass through his fingers. The man gazed across the rolling hills where the serpentine roadway led on to a homestead surrounded by white cypress and apple and pear trees. He heard a child's laughter nearby. There was a flurry in the air as a plump robin alighted on the branch of a scrub pine, cocking his head as if saying, *What are you doing here?* The man cocked his own head and smiled.

A clatter of hoofbeats and shouts panicked the robin into the air.

The man following the bird with his eyes snapped out of his reverie and crashed back to reality. He was not dressed in farmer's cloth, as he had imagined— rather, mounted on his warhorse, he wore the proud armor of Rome's fiercest fighting Legion. The robin flew off over a charred and devastated landscape. Burned, uprooted tree stumps punctuated a field so torn and churned by battle it was a ghastly mire. Fought-over and conquered ground, it was nothing but clotted gray mud and black blood, not a blade or leaf of green left on it.

Past the quagmire, back behind the tree line some-where in the pine forest, the beaten-back Germanic tribal armies were regrouping and preparing for attack.

The man looked over a spectacular and daunting sight. Deployed across the ruts and gulleys, and stretching far into the dim distance, were the trenches, earthworks, and formations of a massive Roman army gearing up for assault—*his* army, the Army of the Danube. Maximus the farmer was Maximus the general for one more battle. One last battle, and he could go home.

Such was his faith in the might of the forces he had amassed on this frigid, sunless afternoon: four full-strength Roman Legions comprising nearly forty thousand troops and auxiliaries dressed for full battle. Ranks of seasoned foot soldiers and cavalry were backed by swarms of longbowmen, slingers, artillery teams, and engineers manning giant *ballistae* and *catapultae*. Syrian archers armed with short bows waited restlessly beside auxiliaries manning machines called *carroballistae,* or Scorpions, that fired multiple crossbow bolts at a single strike. Most fearsome of all in their gleaming, forged black and silver armor were the cream of Roman soldiery, the legionaries, each armed with two throwing spears, an impenetrable bronze and leather shield, and the famed and deadly short sword, the *gladius*. It was an army bristling for battle, itching for war, and thirsty for blood.

A contingent of horses was suddenly upon Maximus, and he had to circle back his mount sharply to avoid the onrush. He raised an arm in salute as a column of armed cavalry swept past in a roar of thundering hooves, harnesses jangling and iron shoes spitting mud and stones. They thrust up their lances in vehement salute to their commander as they clattered down the slope.

Maximus Decimus Meridas, Commanding General

of the Army of the North, wore a white and gray wolf's fur draped across the shoulder plates of his armor as he cantered down among the ranks. It was not for warmth but for the symbolism: that his men might be reminded of the she-wolf, the fierce and nurturing animal that in legend suckled the founders of Rome; reminding the soldiers that they fought for the glory of the Empire.

General Maximus rode past row upon row of grim-faced infantrymen, archers, cavalry, and auxiliaries. The only light any of them saw in the leaden day was in the eye of their commander—a determined gleam that said, *We've walked this road before and have been victorious. And we damn well will again today.*

Small smiles creased the men's dour pre-battle faces as he passed them.

Powerfully built and darkly intense, thirty-year-old Maximus was already a legendary field commander. His legionary officer's armor, with the Wolf of Rome and the crest of his own Felix Cavalry Regiment adorning his breastplate, was imposing but battle-worn, his broadsword stained with the blood and gore of the long campaign. Sweat and grime matted his close-cropped dark hair and short beard, yet in his eyes no trace of fatigue burned, only the hard light of battle. As long as the task was not completed, as long as the Alamanni or the Marcomanni or the Sarmatian tribes stirred unvanquished, he was bound to the trenches. And to his men.

The supreme commanding general of the Army of the Danube and of all the Western armies Maximus might be, but thoughts of his own grandeur never crossed his mind. He believed he was the sum of his men's bravery and loyalty, nothing more.

He moved among his troops, reviewing their readiness. At the line of great *ballistae,* he paused for a word. At his nod, the teams of engineers ran to shift the wheeled, heavy-timbered projectile machines to new angles. He passed a squadron of foot soldiers busy sharpening their stubby, efficacious short swords.

All the while Maximus turned his eyes frequently to the distant tree line, watching and listening for any hint of an attack. He lived in fear of only one thing— getting blindsided, having the enemy onslaught burst on him in full fury before he was primed. The unheard first step, he drilled his men, would be the first knock on the door of their doom.

Wind hissed in the pines and he tilted his head, listening for something specific. Far-off now there was noise—a distant sound of hooves, a few shouted commands carried on the wind. Then nothing.

The commanding general was not alone in turning his eyes frequently toward the distant tree line. All the Roman legionaries—*auxilia* and *numeri* alike— knew that this moment of inertia and lassitude was drawing to a close. Either the glory of battle or the brutal specter of death loomed on the other side of these hours of dread-filled waiting.

Maximus cut through the troops toward the raised command point, where his officers were warming themselves around a campaign brazier, their senses attuned to the mute forest one thousand meters across open ground.

"Still nothing?" Maximus called to Quintus, his trusted second-in-command.

Quintus shook his head. A lean, battle-toughened, scar-faced officer who looked older than his thirty-two years, Quintus Magnus was a regimental commander and a veteran, along with Maximus, of the twelve-year-long German campaign. Other men awaited Maximus's final directives—tribunes, legates, and senior centurions, high officers of the Legions. All of these well-paid, reliable, fearless soldiers were in their twenties and early thirties, but hardened and jaundiced beyond their ages by many years of feral war.

"Not a sign," Quintus said.

Dismounting, Maximus joined the circle and warmed his hands above the brazier. A *tesserarius,* a junior officer, handed him a bowl of steaming soup. He sipped it as they talked in low voices, always keeping one eye on the tree line.

"Snow in the air," Maximus said. "I can smell it."

"Anything's better than this damned German rain," Quintus said, scanning the soggy morass of mire confronting his men.

Maximus glanced at the sky. "How long's he been gone?" he asked.

"Nearly two hours," Valerius said. Valerius was *magister peditum,* Master of Foot, commander of Maximus's infantry divisions. A hulking, bearded man, he gulped at his soup with hands bound with bandages.

"How're the hands?" Maximus said to him in a low tone.

"Stiff," Valerius replied. Valerius had sustained burning-oil wounds on his hands in the previous skirmish with the Germans. The big officer had turned the course of battle by rerouting a stream of flaming oil on a band of Marcomanni about to overrun a squad of legionaries bogged down in mud to their knees. Maximus knew Valerius for the valiant chief centurion he had been for many years. Officers lacking this courage lived short lives or were banished to remote and dismal outposts.

A helmeted, red-plumed cavalry officer galloped up to the foot of the command point, his long sword raised.

"Cavalry in position, General," he called out.

Maximus nodded. "Wait for the signal."

The cavalry officer saluted and wrenched his horse around to return to his post.

Maximus's groom held his nervous mount steady. "Will they fight, sir?" the groom asked quietly.

"We'll know soon enough," the commander replied.

Nearby, the four aquilifers, the chief standard-bearers for each of the four Legions in Maximus's army, waited under their venerated eagle standards. These hallowed emblems—vinewood staffs topped with gilded wing-spread eagles, laurel wreaths, and the blazing insignias for each Legion—embodied the *genius* or undying spirit of each soldier. Attired in their special bearskin uniforms, the aquilifers held their standards straight and eyed Maximus constantly, eager for the signal to raise the emblems and call the men to battle ranks. They, like the rest of the soldiers, were sick to death of the interminable waiting in the freezing mud, and wanted the fight to begin anew.

TWO

Maximus's second-in-command, Quintus, yanked off his helmet and paced restlessly up and down the command post, seething with impatience. The tension had made him irritable. It had been hours! His gaze fell upon the great, sturdy *ballistae*, the stone-throwing and fireball-launching catapults, carefully lined up on the distant tree line, their big wooden front wheels raised on dirt-and-log berms to perfect their launch angles. Quintus yelled at the officer in charge, "I ordered you to move those catapults forward! They're out of range!"

The officer, covered in mud and sweat from having labored with his men to horse the catapults into just the right position, raising and anchoring them, then building the torch fires beside each one for the flaming projectiles, looked tensely from Quintus to Maximus.

The commander responded, in a quiet, neutral voice, "The range is good." He gave Quintus a quick grin, and said, "Don't you agree?" He turned his attention back to his horse, and the catapult officer exhaled in relief.

Quintus took a long breath debating whether to argue the point. He was itching to, but decided to save his bile for the cursed enemy. He turned and stared at the trees again. "What's taking so long?" he growled. "All they have to say is yes or no."

From a lookout far out in the field there came a sudden cry, "He's coming!"

All eyes snapped to the trees. Bodies froze with attention and anticipation. Out of the trees came a horseman galloping toward the Roman lines. The rider disappeared into a dip in the land, then rose again into sight, a bit nearer now, his horse thundering wildly. While the figure was still a great distance off, it became clear there was something strange about the man's carriage, about his loose, jerky posture in the saddle.

Maximus squinted into the glare and haze left from a thousand campfires. His keen eyes saw in a flash of horror and rage what had happened. He let the rider draw a little nearer to be certain. "They say no," Maximus said.

The officers and expectant army surrounding him now saw the horseman close enough to make out what Maximus had realized. The soldier, a high-ranking Roman officer, a centurion entrusted with this mission of great import, was strapped to his horse, headless.

Maximus watched the dead man ride toward them, his torso swaying grotesquely in the saddle, proud black Roman armor and rust-red tunic drenched in streams of blood. Maximus's face was a stone mask, showing nothing but steady concentration. He knew full well what he had to do now. Life was suddenly simple.

"Dear Gods!" Valerius choked.

"I'll crucify them!" Quintus shouted.

Out of the same dense pine woodland far across the no-man's-land, a German tribesman appeared, a huge shaggy man in an animal-skin cloak and primitive battle dress. In one hand he clutched the severed head of the Roman envoy, holding it up by the hair in a bloody display of defiance. He screamed, practically vomiting out his visceral rage at the Roman army

spread out across from him, so enormous it seemed
to stretch from horizon to horizon.

The Roman troops—highly disciplined, battle-
seasoned, and imbued with the mystique of centuries
of superiority—stared back impassively.

The German chieftain swung back his heavily muscled arm and hurled the severed head toward them.
It arced through the air and bounced and rolled grotesquely on the muddy ground.

Maximus shook his head.

"A people should know when they're conquered,"
Quintus rasped with loathing.

Maximus kept his eyes on the enraged tribesman.
"Would you, Quintus?" he said. "Would I?"

Maximus knew the Germans and the seeds of their
rage. Roman Legions had decimated the Alamanni
and Marcomanni and Quadi tribesman's forebears and
driven them from their lands many generations before,
up across the Danube into free Germania and a barren nomadic exile.

Maximus knew the history and grievances of all the
barbarian tribes who had allied together in the most
formidable German confederacy ever seen, bent on driving the Romans out of the rich Rhine-Danube region.
The Chatti, the Alamanni, the Franks, the Roxolani and
other Sarmatian peoples, the Marcomanni of Boiohae-
mum, the Langobardi and Quadi, the Costoboci of Car-
pathia. They were destitute, all of them, their vast
numbers far outstripping the food-supplying capacities
of the frigid, drought-stricken and plague-ridden North.
They were boundless in their hunger for Roman grain
and gold and plunder. They had vengeance and despera-
tion on their side.

Maximus waved away any humanity the enemy
might be supposed to have. *If it must be done*, he
thought to himself, *it will be done well*. The Roman

Legions preceding him had, by might and main, carved and constructed a great empire out of this wilderness and kept it functioning and secure for seven hundred years. He himself had been commander of the besieged and volatile German front now for nearly three years. He would not stop fighting until Rome's enemies were destroyed—until he could leave this portion of the Empire at peace and out of peril.

Maximus roughly clasped Quintus's arm, then Valerius's. "Strength and honor," he said to them.

"Strength and honor," they replied as one.

He pulled on his brass and iron helmet and reached for the reins of his horse, held for him by his groom. He mounted and swung his steed toward the enemy—masses of them visible now, streaming out of the woods.

"Wait for the signal," he called to Quintus, "then unleash hell!" He spurred his mount and galloped off to join the Felix Regiment.

Quintus turned and barked to either side, "Stand by your arms!" Junior officers—*tesserari*—relayed the order down the lines. The command echoed outward in waves across the forty-thousand-man encampment. A rustling rattle of armor and weaponry filled the world, as the immense Roman war machine girded for battle.

"Load the catapults!" Quintus shouted.

The order reverberated down the lines.

"Infantry form up for advance!" he shouted.

The order went out, relayed from prefects to legates to centurions to tesseraries, and the infantry rose and cinched their gear and began to fall in around the eighty different standards in each Legion. Thousands of men, hardened by intense drill and training, found their places unerringly in the ranks under the standards of their own centuries, their battle squads five hundred to six hundred men strong.

"Archers ready," Quintus called.

"Archers ready!" the junior officers shouted down the lines to the auxilliary longbowmen and Syrian archers, nearly ten thousand strong, readying their small, powerful killing bows.

Maximus passed through the ranks at a hard gallop, his heart quickening and his blood rising, his arm raised in Roman salute. Every Roman soldier watched him, lusting for war.

THREE

Explosions of steamy breath pumped from the horses' nostrils as the carriage pounded northward, plunging the Imperial wagons deep into the territory of the savage Alamanni and Marcomanni. Only the endless stone-paved Roman road cleaving the dense forest gave any hint of civilization.

Viae Romanae. The roads of the Roman Empire, like the arteries of a giant, carried power to the extremities. Power in the form of the almighty Legions, in the form of the gold and grain and corn that fueled them, in the form of the Roman laws and edicts and the tough colonial governors and functionaries who enforced them.

The Roman Empire in the second century A.D. girdled the Mediterranean and reached all the way from the Sahara and Egypt to the North Sea, from Gibraltar to farthest Asia Minor. *Pax Romana*—the Roman Peace—bestrode the whole of the developed world, its distant parts cabled together by eight thousand miles of rugged, dependable roads. Phenomenal feats of engineering, with stone substructure and paving, Roman roads were incorruptible by time, destined to be in use two thousand years hence.

But the power that the roads carried—Rome's sway over its 50 million people—was under assault. The onslaught by the amassed Germanic outlanders was unprecedented, and the whole northern campaign hung in the balance. And the vipers that lay coiled within—the conspiracies, treacheries, and corruptions at home—were oozing poison from the heart of the Empire outward. The roads themselves were unassailable, but the power they bespoke was beseiged.

This day, the road to the embattled Rhine-Danube reentrant carried an aspect of stately royalty—and the future.

Or so believed the ambitious young heir, who, swathed in lush furs, hunched impatiently in the armored first wagon of the Imperial caravan. Handsome, athletic, self-hardened in martial virtues, twenty-eight-year-old Lucius Aurelius Commodus found himself two weeks' fast travel out of Rome, nearing the front lines. He was in the company of his elegant, slightly older sister Annia Lucilla. Both were traveling under Imperial command.

"Do you think he's really dying?" Commodus asked, his breath condensing in a frozen fog on the icy air.

"He's been dying for ten years," Lucilla said. She was beautiful and patrician, garbed in the furs and silks of privilege, and every bit as formidable a presence as her brother.

"I think he's really dying this time," Commodus said, swatting away his misted breath. "He has to be bled every night now."

"How do you know that?" Lucilla inquired, steadying herself against the wagon's lurch as it rumbled over the highway.

Commodus gazed out at the passing forest at a line of wounded *auxilae,* supplementary Roman troops, tramping along the roadside. "I've been so informed," he said.

Lucilla arched an eyebrow.

"If he weren't really dying," he said, "he wouldn't have sent for us."

"Maybe he just misses us," she replied, allowing a smile.

"And the senators," Commodus added, nodding with annoyance toward the following wagons. "He wouldn't have summoned them as well if—"

"Peace, Commodus," Lucilla said. "After two weeks on the road, your incessant scheming is hurting my head."

The handsome young man stared off into the distant countryside, envisioning glorious days on the horizon. "No . . . ," he said, coming and sitting near his sister. "He's made his decision. He's going to announce it." He lay back, seeing a congenial world unfolding in his mind's eye. "He will name me."

Lucilla looked at him with amused eyes, noting the smile creeping over his daydreaming face, and the flush of anticipation in his voice.

"The first thing I shall do," he said, "is honor him with games worthy of his majesty."

"Right now, the first thing I shall do," Lucilla yawned, "is have a hot bath."

The wagon rumbled to a halt. Voices called back and forth outside. Commodus stepped out on the rear platform and looked down at his accompanying mounted guard, a cavalry officer of the *Cohortes Praetoriae*, the elite and powerful civil guard of Rome.

Behind the praetorian, laborers in a road gang bent to the task of keeping the Roman highway in repair. The colonial engineer in charge gawked at the eminent presence on the tailgate of the wagon. He stepped forward for a closer look.

"We seem to be almost there, sire," the mounted praetorian said.

Commodus called past him to the colonial engineer, "Where's the Emperor?"

The engineer gaped at his Imperial trappings, stunned to realize the distinction of the personage above him. He fell to one knee in a gesture of great deference. "At the front, sire," he answered.

"Is the battle won?" Commodus asked.

"Don't know, sire," the engineer said. "They've been gone for nineteen days. The wounded are still coming in."

Commodus tossed back his furs. "My horse!" he barked to his officer. "Take me to my father." Beneath his furs, Commodus wore a striking, polished set of *lorica segmentata,* the traditional forged armor of the Legions. He cut a brilliant figure, poised and impatient, as magnificent as the impressive stallion that was led up to him.

"Take my sister to the camp," Commodus ordered another of the *praetoriani*, and turned to Lucilla as she emerged from the back of the wagon onto the platform. He reached out one hand with a boyish grin. "Kiss," he said.

She caught the tips of his fingers, just a touch to send him on his way. He pivoted and made a single leap to mount his horse. He cantered away, followed by a clattering escort spurring to catch up with him.

Lucilla watched him go, bemused. She glanced down at the motley road gang still kneeling in deference. "Civilization at last," she said dryly to herself. "Gods preserve us."

FOUR

The strong bones in his face showed through the exhausted features of age, the clear lines of character undiminished by the years.

Marcus Aurelius, Emperor of Rome, sat on his horse in erect military posture, cloaked in the purple and gold of his supreme rank, staring down at the troops forming in battle lines below. His face was burned brown by a lifetime of sun and wind, his flowing hair and cropped beard thinned and whitened now, but still majestic. Only his eyes betrayed that he was ailing. A close observer might see that under the Imperial purple cloak he was propped upright on his horse with thick leather straps attached to a metal brace extending from the back of his saddle.

Even now in his frailty, he was not to be trifled with. The list of men who had done so, and had thus come to languish in exiled obscurity or in their graves, was long. He understood how to get power, how to keep it, and how to wield it. He was the philosopher king, perhaps the only true one in the history of the Western world.

More attuned to musing and writing on the nature and foibles of human nature, Marcus Aurelius had nonetheless been chosen by fate to lead the greatest political power ever conceived on earth—and, ironically, to spend much of his reign at war. He took an

Empire expanded to its fullest reach by Trajan, an Emperor before him, and amplified its greatness. He had fortified its six thousand miles of frontier, fought off its resurgent enemies, and created an internal state administered with a degree of stability, probity, and humanity. Yet he was nearing the end of his allotted time in the arena and had his eyes on the last tasks: his legacy, the great responsibility and burden he would pass on to the next holder of the Imperial scepter.

Marcus was impatient for the battle to be joined. The old juices had begun to course again in his veins with the trumpets' blare. But he knew too that his time for battles was limited. The Alamanni and Marcomanni had amassed a horrendous force for a desperate and frightening final push. If Marcus's Legions could prevail here and crush them mercilessly, peace would reign for many years on this last unpacified front. And the Emperor could, with an easier conscience, proceed to his final and perhaps most important function: shaping the future of his revered Roman Empire by naming a successor.

The Emperor had prepared his legionaries in spirit for this battle, having moments before performed the ritual obeisance to the martial gods as centuries of tradition bid.

The entire army, every clerk and cartwright, every squad of foot soldier and horseman, every centurion, every cohort, had congregated around the camp altar. The high-ranking *aquiliferi* of the Legions and the lesser-ranked *signiferi* for the Centuria clustered their standards close to the altar for all the men to see. The trumpets sounded the Imperial salute as Marcus Aurelius appeared in their midst and commenced the sacrifice to the chief Roman God, Jupiter. And while Marcus privately held no credence with such tripe—

battles were won with superior forces, arms, and strategy, not divine intercession—the men needed to believe. So the Emperor—as *Pontifex Maximus,* the Chief Priest—did not stint in the fervor of his performance.

Intoning an ancient solemn text enlisting the complicity of Jupiter and all the Gods, the Emperor sprinkled oil and perfume on the sacred fire. Priests felled a white ox with a battle-axe, opening its belly and inspecting the organs and entrails. It was found that the beast's liver, heart, and intestines were in right relation to one another and properly situated within the animal. Marcus proclaimed it ordained that the Gods would smile upon the Romans in battle this day. A raucous cheer erupted above a deafening rattle of armor and pounding of feet from the ranks.

"Remember, to a Roman, an honorable death is better than a lifetime of shame!" Marcus cried out to the assembly. "Are you ready for war?"

Thrice he asked them that question, and thrice the answer came back, "We are ready for war!"

The trumpets rang out three times, then three times again. The legionaries responded with a clamor of armor and a roar of battle boasts and cheers. The congregation broke up and soldiers repaired to their standards, hooting and shouting and goading one another to exultation and valor.

Sitting his horse now above the din and battle shouts ringing out below, Marcus Aurelius waited. His mounted staff behind him shifted in their saddles. Together they looked down upon the spectacle of the mightiest army ever invented by man, now restlessly forming up for battle.

FIVE

Astride his horse, his cavalry regiment all around him, Maximus stood atop a hill overlooking his assembled forces. Breath flared from his horse's nostrils into the icy air. Cold sunlight flashed and glittered off of the legionaries' segmented armor and ready swords. The entire vast army, arrayed in tense formation before him, watched their commander, awaiting the signal—all of them glancing frequently at the distant woods where thousands of shaggy men were now visible, the front line of an uncountable multitude.

On Maximus's right waited a mounted archer. Beside the archer, a foot soldier held a torch of burning straw and pitch.

The commander-in-chief made a last check of his men's positions: At the forefront crouched three great ranks of *numeri*, thousands of non-Roman, half-savage infantry recruits with their own crude weapons; flanking them were two regiments of similar tribal cavalry, armed with a sword and three spears each.

Behind them were eight cohorts of *auxilae*, recruits from the border provinces with their special talents as archers and slingers, skilled as well on horseback with their long slashing swords.

Disposed behind them in an immense arc, positioned for the killing blow, were three full Roman Legions standing side by side, the fourth held in reserve to the left. They were the elite—superbly trained, disciplined, well armored, and shielded—feared for the ruthless efficiency with which they wielded the two-edged *gladius*.

The dark-garbed barbarian force back among the trees, far across the wasteland, began to move, thousands of them, and then more thousands, with their wild scraggly hair and animal-skin battle cloaks. They made feinting lunges toward the Romans, brandishing their weapons, starting their war chant: *"Barritus! Barritus! Barritus!"*

Maximus bent down in the saddle and scraped up a handful of earth without dismounting. Righting himself, he rubbed the earth between his hands as if it were a solemn ceremony. It was his standard ritual, a final act before battle, familiar to all those who had ever fought beside him. He did it automatically, his attention focused on the growing barbarian horde.

His fighting men saw the gesture, and a murmur ran through the ranks as men nudged each other. The lowliest foot soldier among them knew the sign—they had seen it many times before. The moment of battle was upon them. Their mouths dried, their pulses began to race, they made their desperate final entreaties to their own gods, and all up and down the lines the soldiers began to pound on their shields with their swords, a deafening drumming, watching for the first act of battle.

Maximus nodded to the mounted archer on his right. The archer nocked a cloth-tipped, pitch-dipped arrow, and the foot soldier with the torch set it aflame. The archer stretched back the powerful longbow to its limit and let fly. All the cavalry looked up, tracing the arc of the flaming arrow as it sang through the air.

To the left, at the command point near the Emperor's salient, Quintus's heart leapt as he spied the fiery arrow rising into the sky. He turned to the lines of longbowmen and Scorpions, and to the battery of mighty *ballistae* ranked to his right. "Now!" Quintus shouted with the incomprehensible joy of battle echoing in his voice.

The heavy catapults, loaded and strained back to maximum tension on their tightened springs of rope, were loosened. Rocketing into the air, a hundred bulbous terra-cotta pots rose over the trees. Quintus counted off the seconds as they flew.

". . . two . . . three . . . four . . . Now!" he cried out.

Sixty Scorpions unleashed their multifold fusillades of deadly bolts, sending them streaking under the arc of the clay pots, on the same heading.

"Archers, fire!" Quintus called out.

Hundreds of archers, poised with their flaming pitch-and-straw arrows fully lighted, released their bowstrings. A ragged line of fire traced across the sky.

Maximus and his cavalry watched the bomblike pots sailing high overhead toward the trees.

Quintus and all his men followed the flight of the missiles in silent expectation.

The shrieking swarm of crossbow bolts raced through the air on a flat trajectory and intersected the arc of the clay pots as they fell toward the trees. The speeding bolts shattered the pots, creating starbursts of falling pitch. The wave of flaming arrows passed through the curtains of raining pitch, and a crescendo of explosions lit the sky. Blazing oil fell like brimstone from Hades into the sheltering trees where the barbarian army was poised.

The Romans waited, listening . . .

Then the screaming began.

Out of the crackling inferno of the forest burst hundreds of shrieking German tribesmen, madly trying to strip away the liquid fire eating their skin and hair.

They staggered and fell, rolling on the muddy ground in agony.

Then a great tidal wave of fur-draped warriors swept out of the trees, through and over the immolated front line and straight toward the Romans, waving their spears and axes and screaming insanely.

The savage first charge of the last desperate battle was under way.

Quintus raised his sword arm and signaled the advance, crying out, *"Roma Aeterna!"*

Battle trumpets sounded.

The soldiers responded, *"Roma Invicta!"* and began to move.

The forefront army of Roman *numeri* marched out to meet the onslaught. The German savages, still pouring out of the forest in one unending howling swarm, advanced on the *numeri* like storm waves crashing on the shore. They barely slowed as they met the Roman first line, shredding through them and running forward, undeterred.

Quintus signaled again, and a second trumpet call sounded.

The Syrian archers and slingers fired, and the deadly barrage cut a great swath from the enemy vanguard. An even more massive wave of tribesmen replaced them as quickly as they fell, closing now on a line of Roman foot soldiers stretching out in either direction. The disciplined Roman infantry, armed with javelins, their right arms drawn back, stood stock-still.

The screaming barbarians came on at lumbering speed—one hundred yards . . . seventy yards . . . forty . . . thirty . . .

A third trumpet call rang out.

The soldiers' arms whipped forward. At the same instant, the rearmed *carroballistae* of all three deployed Legions unleashed a storm of iron bolts. The sky darkened with two thousand javelins and five thousand iron arrows. German savages pitched over and crumpled in heaps up and down the line, bodies piling up, creating confusion and at last a slight break in their ferocious charge.

But it proved to be only a momentary break. Incredibly, another wave of savages broke over the fallen bodies in numbers larger than before—a seemingly unending onslaught.

Maximus, standing high in the saddle, witnessed the masses of men pouring out of the woods like a swollen river. It looked to him as though all of Free Germany was streaming through this narrow point in Danubia, trying to burst through into the Elysian Fields of the Roman Empire.

The moment for the Felix Regiment had arrived. The horses shifted skittishly on all sides, sensing approaching havoc. Maximus pulled taut on his reins. "Steady," he said to his mount.

He then drew his sword. "Soldiers! Brothers!" he shouted. "Are you ready?"

"Aye!" his cavalrymen shouted back, positioned in their line shoulder to shoulder.

"Hold the formation! Match my speed!" Maximus shouted, reining in his straining horse. "If you find you're on your own, riding through green fields with sun on your face—you're in Elysium, and you're dead!"

His veterans roared with glee, happy that the decisive time had come. There was no more agonizing, only skull-splitting action.

Over their guffaws, Maximus shouted, "And we'll all be joining you soon enough." He raised his sword high, feeling the exhilaration of all-out battle. He looked young and free and joyous—the pure warrior.

"Three weeks from now, I'll be harvesting my

grapes!" he shouted. "Imagine where you will be! And it will be so. What we do now echoes in eternity!"

Maximus dug his heels into his horse's flanks and leapt forward, leading the charge. The Felix Regiment, shouting *"Mars Ultor!"*—"Mars the Avenger!"—spurred their mounts and raced at his side.

Building up speed, they cut deep into the left side of the German reinforcements in a sharp flanking maneuver, crying *"Cide!"*—"Kill!"

At full gallop among the barbarian foot soldiers, they pierced with their spears and slashed with their long swords. They split the German advance in two, and brought it to a standstill, then turned them. Slowly they drove one contingent of tribesmen straight back into the burning forest, hammering at them, pursuing them relentlessly over the uneven murky ground. Finding himself trapped between two Germans, Maximus wheeled his horse and slashed his sword in a roundhouse swing so powerful he cleaved through both Germans and almost pulled over his horse. He galloped forward to gash his sword through one Quadi warrior who was about to bring his axe down on one of his men, then plunged his dagger into the neck of another Quadi with his left hand.

In the center of the melee, the Germans were fighting for their lives, exacting appalling damage. A young centurion at the head of a unit of surrounded auxiliary infantry rallied his men from bloody extinction by plunging into a knot of savages, crying "Jupiter! Jupiter!" and slashing down one barbarian after another. His men drew strength and fought back, gaining ground. But with a broad swipe of the enemy chief's huge iron sword, the centurion was nearly split from top to bottom. The youngest auxiliaries began to fall back, panicking and breaking formation. The fight degenerated into a muddy, frenzied slaughter.

From the right, behind a screen of auxiliaries and a cover barrage of artillery arrows, the first of the Legions had moved into position. Without fanfare they wheeled, five thousand men strong behind their great bronze-rimmed curved shields, and began to advance. They advanced in a cool, implacable, terrible manner, their swords leveled.

At the left rear, out of the flaming trees at full gallop, burst Maximus and the howling Felix Regiment, bearing down on the German center with swords whirling. The Germans turned in terror, caught between two walls of death. Maximus's horsemen were then upon them, cutting them down savagely.

In the rage of the battle, Maximus spun his horse, swinging his sword to great advantage from his superior height, felling tribesmen on one side and the other. Nearly a dozen enemy had fallen before a spear stabbed through Maximus's horse's neck, sending the animal pitching suddenly to the earth. The commander sailed over his horse's head, crashing to the rutted ground.

He rolled and clattered to his feet, still fighting. Flaming arrows sang overhead and a firepot exploded over the enemy's center position. Falling flames silhouetted the combatants who fought on in the midst of a fierce inferno.

On the ground Maximus was everywhere, exhorting his men, skirmishing, managing to dodge gruesome axes and sharp blades by dint of always getting in the first cut.

He charged among the battle-crazed mob of Germans, slashing with desperate might to get to a signifier who was staggering with a splinter of a spear stuck deep in his back, still holding his standard upright. Maximus dragged the dying signifier to the feet of a medical orderly, plunged the staff of his standard into the muddy brow of an incline, and shouted to the man's unit not to let their standard—their *genius*—fall into the hands of the enemy. The auxiliaries saw the banner and fought their way toward it. They formed up under the eagle and followed the lead of their commander, defending their position with fury. For if they fell, so might the power of Rome in this far, bloodied outpost of the Empire.

SIX

There was an aura about the commander of the Northern armies when he fought—men felt it, ally and foe the same. He was a beautifully efficient machine of war: He fought smart, wasting not an ounce of energy, economizing his moves, saving his breath, and looking for his spots. He saw openings, angles, and trajectories and got his horrendous killing blow in before the enemy had time to draw back his weapon.

But more than that was the searing core of self-belief, the confidence that he could vanquish any of Rome's foes no matter the odds.

On the right flank, the legionaries were advancing behind the work of their short, lethal twin-edged *gladius*. In disciplined formation, one yard apart, they marched upon the wild tribesmen calmly and relentlessly, warding off blows with curved shield and toughened leather armor, aggressively delivering thrust after uncannily accurate thrust into enemy flesh. The helmetless, armorless tribal warriors facing this juggernaut—with fresh troops coming at them on two sides at once—began to tire, break apart, and fall back, the heated rush of battle quickly evaporating.

At last, and not without grievous loss, the Roman army began to beat back their relentless enemy. Superior in training, discipline, firepower, and leadership, the Army of the Danube was grinding down the large

German force, turning their crazed bloodlust into weeping exhaustion.

Sensing the tide turning in his forces' favor, Maximus pulled back to better command his troops. Sorting out the chaos, he signaled his men where to rally, where to fall back in aid of auxiliaries in stubborn hand-to-hand clashes. He directed small cavalry charges, as several horsemen lined up knee to knee and were sent slashing into groups of Germans still gamely trying to fight.

Where Marcomanni and Alamanni chieftains fell, loyal tribesmen often stayed to fight to the death alongside their leaders. Maximus and his fighters took note of such bravery, but did not stay their swords for an instant. Answering to their training, they expertly cut down every enemy standing, even those who had fallen and still had life left in them.

With the wall of unstoppable legionaries moving ever forward, killing everything in their reach, the barbarians lost heart. First a few of the Roxolani broke and ran, then a few Marcomanni, then more and more—the Chatti, the Langobardi, the Alamanni—turned and fled as they saw their fellow combatants in retreat. It became a flood of men choosing life, wanting to escape the terrible slaughter.

Maximus walked freely now among the dead and dying. Beginning to feel the juices of battle drain away, and then the waves of profound exhaustion that always followed bloody combat, he let his sword arm swing at his side as he stepped over corpses.

Out of the bodies littering the gore-soaked ground rose one wild German. Horribly wounded, feeling himself in death's embrace, he saw the chance to take the enemy chieftain with him to the great beyond. His sword raised, he charged at Maximus at a moment when the commander had his back turned, calling an order to one of his officers. Maximus saw the look come over his officer's face, and, lacking even half an instant to assess the threat, he swung his great sword round in one mighty sweep and decapitated the attacker. The sheer power of his swing carried the arc of the sword past the man and *thock!*—buried it deep into the trunk of a scorched pine.

Leaning against the tree, depleted, Maximus didn't have the strength left to pull the sword out of the trunk.

Marcus Aurelius, strapped to his horse atop the low command hill, flanked by two protective cohorts of Praetorian Guardsmen, watched as the confusing fray of battle slowly resolved into a Roman victory.

It was a bloody business, and though it usually turned out in the Romans' favor, it didn't always. In the reign of the Emperor Augustus, a Germanic tribe called the Cherusci had dealt the Romans an historic defeat, annihilating three entire Legions in an ambush in a swamp in the Teutoburg Forest. A humiliated Augustus was tormented with night sweats about it until his death. In the two decades of Marcus's reign, his Legions had suffered only two great defeats: one at the hands of the Marcomanni and Quadi, and the other by Carpathian Costoboci. The latter had overrun lower Danubia, marched deep into Greece and plundered Eleusis. But Marcus Aurelius's armies shared a trait with all Roman Legions—they never gave up. They reformed and came back to fight again and again. Ultimately, they crushed the marauders and drove them back into their own lands.

Many days and seasons and years would pass, Marcus hoped, before Rome's Legions would have to wage war again. The field was strewn with enemy corpses, black and filthy blood fouling their slashed furs and tunics. Were enough corpses made today to convince the warring tribes at last to sign treaties and live with the Roman frontiers in peace? Or would it just be the peace of stalemate, festering until famine or plague or a maniacal tribal chief drove them to cross borders and attack peaceful farms and towns again?

Marcus prayed it would not be within his lifetime. He was fairly certain, in the failing state in which he felt himself to be, that he would not live to see another campaign. For that he was grateful.

He turned and indicated to his staff that he wished to ride away.

Maximus stood looking at his sword imbedded in the trunk of the pine tree. He was splattered with mud and gore, sweating, trying to catch his breath. His pounding heart was gradually slowing down. The shouts and clangs of battle were beginning to recede, replaced by low groans and sudden shrieks of anguish from men lying wounded and dying. The acrid smell of burning pitch filled the air, along with the stink of rent flesh and spilled blood.

Perched cheekily on the hilt of Maximus's suspended sword was a plump robin. Could it possibly be the same bird he had seen before battle exploded? Maximus gazed at the bird, and shook his head once. He gently reached up to the sword hilt. Startled, the robin flew away. He jerked the sword out of the tree.

Maximus turned and looked over the onetime forest meadow, now a garish scene from the bowels of Hades.

Roman surgeons were moving in with pallet teams to bind up and carry away the severely wounded. Auxiliary infantry moved over the gulleys and rises, probing enemy bodies with swords and spears for any

Germans left alive. Any body that moved was executed with a quick stab.

Roman soldiers in agony moaned and called for water and medical aid on all sides. It would take the next three days just to bury all the dead.

Maximus made his way back toward the command point, weaving through the grisly field, stepping around inert forms. Frequently he stopped and grasped the arm of a wounded comrade, offering words of solace, encouragement, and gratitude. He beckoned the surgeons to attend to each one of them in turn.

He came to a low hill where orderlies and auxiliaries were grouping dead Roman soldiers, preparing them for the graves the engineers were digging. As they carried more bodies to the hillside and lay them down side by side, Maximus knelt with the dead, taking stock of the human carnage.

"Let the flowers never fade," he said to himself. "Let the sun always be warm on your back. But better than this, All the beloved dead returned to you, as you return to them. Embrace them. You've come home at last."

He noticed, as he finished, that the orderlies and soldiers were all beginning to kneel in postures of respect, all facing the same point behind him.

"You proved your valor once again, Maximus," a voice said. "Let us hope it is for the last time."

Maximus turned to find the Emperor standing over him.

"There's no one left to fight, sire," Maximus said, rising to his feet and bowing slightly.

"There are always people to fight, Maximus," Marcus said. "More glory."

Maximus looked over the field of the slain and mutilated, and shook his head. "The glory is theirs, Caesar," he said.

"How then," Marcus said, "am I to reward Rome's greatest general?"

"Let me go home," Maximus replied without hesitation.

"Ah, home . . . ," Marcus said. He raised one arm to indicate to Maximus that he would like his support. Maximus at once moved to his side and held the Emperor's arm. They walked back across the battlefield together, listening to the cries of misery on all sides. The Imperial entourage of *praetoriani* and other subalterns followed closely, ready to protect the Imperial life.

All eyes followed the flowing purple cloak and white hair and chiseled patrician features of the elderly monarch. They saw how painfully and slowly he moved, and most of the soldiers realized they were probably seeing him in their midst for the last time. Nor were they likely to see so good an Emperor again in their lifetimes, in a realm notorious for elevating fools and degenerates to the throne.

Marcus Aurelius and his victorious general passed along the road lined with exhausted and wounded soldiers lying back against a hillside, drained of all energy. Upon spying the two personages, the whole hillside of fighters abruptly hauled themselves to their feet and raised their swords in silent homage.

"They honor you, Caesar," Maximus said with a slight bow of his head.

"I think it is you, Maximus," the Emperor said. "I believe they honor you."

Maximus looked across the mass of brave men, and as he raised his own sword in salute, a hearty, emotional cheer burst from the men.

At that instant, Crown Prince Commodus, in his impressive, shiny, untouched *lorica segmentata* armor and astride his fine horse, cantered into view at the head of his flashy, dozen-man Praetorian Guard escort.

Commodus saw and heard the rousing tribute the troops were paying Maximus. A flush of rank envy ran through him; who was this Spaniard to elicit such devotion from Roman legionaries who rightfully owed their full allegiance to the Emperor and his line?

He pushed the thought aside and put on his best face as he galloped up to Marcus and Maximus. "Have I missed it?" he said, leaping from his saddle. "Have I missed the battle?"

"You've missed the war," Marcus said drily. "We're done here."

Commodus awkwardly embraced his father. "Father, congratulations," he said. "I shall sacrifice a hundred bulls to honor your triumph."

"Let the bulls live and honor Maximus," Marcus said. "He won the battle."

"General," Commodus said, turning. "Rome salutes you, and I embrace you as a brother." He opened his arms and clutched Maximus, even more awkwardly. "It has been too long. What is it? Ten years, my old friend?"

"Highness," Maximus said.

"Your Spaniards seem invincible," the young prince said. "May the Gods favor the Felix Regiment now and always." He turned to Marcus. "Here, Father, take my arm."

Marcus let his hand rest on his son for a moment. Then, with a gentle smile, said, "I think perhaps I should leave you now."

Commodus waved for Marcus's horse. A groom ran forward with the mount, and several of the Praetorian Guard carefully helped the old man into the saddle. They fussed around him, positioning the straps, adjusting the purple raiment until he held up his hand for them to stop.

He looked to Maximus. Maximus crossed quickly to him, and adjusted the support straps.

"So much for the glory of Rome," Marcus said, smiling. Without a word to his son, he nodded, and the horse was slowly led away.

Commodus and Maximus watched the Emperor go for a long moment, each lost in his own thoughts.

Maximus mused with deepest sympathies for the old man, knowing the depth of his well-meaning nature. High on the longtime monarch's list of life rules, Maximus knew, was Marcus's exhortation to himself "not to be too deeply dyed with the purple." When Marcus returned to Rome for his Triumphs, and was paraded along the Sacra Via with his legionaries and his captives, wagons piled high with plunder, he always made sure to protect himself against vainglory. As his chariot passed among cheering, screaming, idolizing crowds, he ordered the servant behind him—whose job it was to hold the laurel wreath above his head—to whisper in his ear, "Never forget you are only a man."

Marcus's Imperial life had been filled with extreme and anguishing burdens and, he had confided to Maximus, almost more than he had been able to bear. In this life, this fleeting visit to an alien land, he believed, the least we should do is carry on self-reliantly and with decency and responsibility toward our fellow travelers.

Maximus would remember the good man's philosophical mind far longer than the details of any of the great military campaigns he had waged and won for the glory of Rome.

Commodus's thoughts were elsewhere: He stood fuming with agitation that the old man had not clasped him to his bosom and swept him along with him for a private communing. He swung himself back onto his handsome horse and spurred it away, followed by his escort.

SEVEN

Under a starless night sky, Maximus emerged from a ward in the hospital tent city that sprawled over two acres, housing the thousands of men wounded in the battle. He grieved to know that many of the gravely injured suffering in the tents would never be whole again, and many more would die before the sun came up. Some lucky ones would be retired with pensions to one or another of the frontier communities populated by generations of ex-legionaries, never to fight again.

But Roman fighting men were too valuable to be allowed to die of wounds or disease, he reassured his fallen comrades. Roman medical officers were good surgeons, armed with uncanny knowledge of medicines made with herbs. Many of the even seriously wounded troops, in prime shape from their intense training, would recover and return to their regiments and to full legionary status.

Maximus joined a weary surgeon washing his hands before a fire. Orderlies and medics on all sides ministered to countless lesser casualties resting on the ground—splinters of wood or metal that needed to be plucked out, minor punctures and slices that needed some herbal unguent and a rough stitch or two. Maximus nodded his departure to the surgeon and moved away into the main part of the immense Roman encampment, a sea of tents among which thousands of campfires gleamed, sending columns of smoke skyward.

The grand mess tent was a scene of high energy, a heady swirl of noise. It was crowded with regimental officers still in their battle garb, still filthy with caked-on mud and blood—their badges of glory. It was the celebration of their victory, and wine and ale flowed in torrents. Everyone was drinking to the Gods, to their officers, to each other, raising cups in swaddled hands, laughing, and shouting. They celebrated the sweet taste of lives narrowly pulled back from death's gaping maw. They toasted the recently dead and wished them godspeed to the Elysian Fields they hoped to see someday themselves—but thankfully not today.

Marcus sat in a throne-chair in a central position and received visitors. Two senators, Falco and Gaius, bowed before him. They were fish out of water in their august, pristine senatorial togas. They had traveled in the same caravan that had brought Commodus from distant Rome.

"Hail, Marcus Aurelius," Falco said, bowing low. He was a cropped-haired, stern-faced city tough with eyes as shiny and opaque as onyx.

"Stand up, senators," Marcus said with a dry smile. "That unfamiliar posture doesn't suit you."

"We live in supplication to your glory," Gaius said, smiling warmly. He was a youthful country Italian with dark curly hair, who kept an up-to-date file on the dirty dealings of every member of the Senate.

"All the while conspiring with that fat man in Rome," Marcus said. "How is the old monster?"

"Senator Gracchus is hale, sir," Gaius replied.

"Still damning me to the four winds?" Marcus queried.

"Still eager for your triumphant return to Rome, Caesar," Gaius said.

Maximus entered the tent. As soon as he appeared, soldierly arms reached out to embrace him, and ale cups were thrust in his hands. Smiling, taking a sip here and a gulp there and hailing each man by name, he pushed his way through the throng. He grabbed one man by the nape, an *optio,* a mid-ranking officer whom he had seen save the life of an aquilifer that day, and whispered to him that he was in line for the *corona civica,* the wreath of oak leaves that was Rome's highest battle medal, and that he would be promoted to centurion immediately. He left the man with his mouth agape, struggling for words of thanks.

He pushed past his second-in-command, Quintus, and a group of legionaries all trying to tell their battle stories at once. Quintus stopped talking and raised his arms at the sight of his commander.

"Still alive! The Gods must love you!" Quintus and Maximus said together. Maximus laughed, and he and Quintus embraced with rough elation. Maximus pushed on, with Quintus and the officers trailing after him.

On the far side, through the crush of bodies and a forest of heads, Maximus could see Marcus Aurelius in a group of men, receiving visitors, and it was with the old man that he most wanted to share this moment.

As he drew nearer, he saw Commodus at the Emperor's side, along with the two senators, Falco and Gaius. Commodus caught sight of Maximus and pointed him out to the others.

Maximus paused as more of his men insisted on toasting him.

"Back to barracks, General? Or to Rome?" asked

Valerius, the burly infantry commander with the bandaged hands.

"I'm going home," Maximus said. "To wife, and son, and the harvest."

"Maximus the farmer!" Quintus said laughing. "I still have difficulty imagining that."

"Dirt washes off easier than blood, Quintus," Maximus said.

Commodus, Gaius, and Falco approached Maximus.

"Here he is," Commodus said. "The hero of the war!"

"Highness," Maximus said. He did not warm to Commodus's pandering. He also did not appreciate being lionized within earshot of his brave officers, whose courage and loyalty were the backbone of his command.

"Senator Gaius . . . Senator Falco," Commodus said, introducing the senators to Maximus. "Beware of this Gaius," he said to Maximus with a grin. "He'll pour a honeyed potion in your ear, you'll wake up one day and all you'll say is 'Republic, republic, republic.' "

They all laughed, including Maximus, who chuckled as he bowed to the senators.

"Why not?" Gaius said. "Rome was founded as a republic."

"And in a republic, the Senate has the power," Commodus said. "And Senator Gaius isn't influenced by *that*, of course." He shook his head with mock rue.

"Where do you stand, General?" Falco said. "Emperor or Senate?"

"Soldiers have the advantage of being able to look their enemy in the eye . . . Senator," Maximus said, flatly refusing the game.

Gaius's brow arched as he assessed Maximus in person, this bloodstained warrior whose magnetism and acumen he had heard much about. Now he was getting a firsthand whiff of the bold head and forthright heart of the man. "With an army behind you," the senator said pointedly, "you could be extremely political."

Gaius's remark was not just idle flattery; he was shrewdly envisioning a possibly interesting future for the military man, based purely on Roman political realities.

It was an ill-kept secret that although the Senate had the nominal power to elect the man who would lead the Empire, it was in fact little more than a rubber-stamp approval. The real power resided in whichever strong man had the loyalty and control of the army.

"Senatus Populusque Romanus" or "SPQR," as it was embroidered on the standards of the Legions—was the motto for the original government of and by the Senate and the Roman people. The elected republic had lasted five hundred long years, until all hell broke loose with the assassination of Julius Caesar in 44 B.C. At that point, when it became a choice between nonstop civil war and the safe streets and full bellies that powerful Caesar Augustus offered, the Senate opted for domestic tranquility. It "elected" Augustus the first Emperor of Rome, and dictators had ruled ever since.

But the draw of a senatorial republic was still a powerful one to the Roman people, especially when the Emperor was a mad dog or a fool. So when the prospect of a change in Emperors loomed, everybody got nervous, and started hedging their bets.

"I warned you," Commodus said to Maximus, laughing. "Now I shall save you." He took Maximus's arm and led him firmly aside.

As the two men moved away together, a pair of cobalt female eyes could be seen looking through an opening in the wall of the officers' mess tent. The eyes followed closely the movements of Maximus.

Commodus led Maximus to a quieter corner and spoke in low tones. "Times are changing, General," he said. "I'm going to need good men like you."

"How can I be of service, Highness?" Maximus said.

"You're a man who knows what it is to command," Commodus said. "You give your orders, the orders are obeyed, the battle is won."

Maximus remained silent. He looked at the Emperor's son with a steady gaze.

"They scheme and squabble and flatter and deceive," Commodus continued, looking back at the senators, who were busy deferentially plying the Emperor with amusing stories from the Forum and the Palatine Hill. "We must save Rome from the politicians, my friend." He put a hand on Maximus's shoulder, and continued the flattering game as if they were old friends. "I can count on you when the time comes?" he asked.

"When your father releases me, I return to Spain. Sire," Maximus said firmly. He wanted to ensure his statement was taken at face value, and not mistaken for an affront to the Imperial family.

"Home? Ah! *Leave*," Commodus said. "Well, no one's earned it more." He smiled, then he leaned close and murmured, "Don't get too comfortable. I may call on you before long."

He feigned ending the conversation on that note, grabbing up two pots of ale and handing one to Maximus. He offered the general a silent toast.

Then, as though in afterthought, with an open, casual tone, he said, "Lucilla is here. Did you know?" He threw Maximus a quick look to gauge his reaction. He thought he saw a flicker in the general's eyes.

"She's not forgotten you," Commodus said. "And now you're the great hero."

Satisfied he had his hooks into Maximus, he turned to saunter back to the Imperial presence, and saw his father being helped out of the tent by his body slaves. "Caesar retires early tonight," he said, bemused.

When he turned back, Maximus had gone. Now a flicker of something crossed his own eyes. Uncertainty. Irritation. Calculation. Where did the great general's ultimate loyalties lie? Calm self-assurance and trust in the benevolence of others' motives were not traits bred into Commodus by his life in the snake pit of the Roman elite. He took a long draught of ale to quiet his incurable anxiety.

EIGHT

Marcus's slaves helped him out of the officers' mess and into a tent corridor, a passageway that doubled as a sort of Imperial anteroom. Looking around, he saw his daughter Lucilla at the opening in the tent wall with her lady-in-waiting. Clearly they had been watching the goings-on. He half smiled. "If only you'd been born a man . . . ," he said.

Lucilla turned to him. He left his slaves and went to embrace her. "Father," she said with a warm smile, and kissed the old man's cheek with restrained affection.

"What a Caesar you would have made," he said thoughtfully. "You would have been strong. I wonder if you would have been just."

"I would have been what you taught me to be," Lucilla replied.

He smiled with a raised brow. She took his arm and they slowly walked down the tent corridor.

"How was the journey?" Marcus asked.

"Long. Uncomfortable," Lucilla said. "Why have I come?"

"I need your help," her father said. "With your brother."

"Of course."

"He loves you. He always has." Marcus came to a

weary stop, and turned his face to hers. "He's going to need you more than ever."

Lucilla studied her father, unsure of what to say.

"No more. It's not a night for politics," Marcus said. "It's a night for an old man and his daughter to look at the moon together." As they continued down the corridor, he added with unaffected irony, "Let's pretend that you are a loving daughter and I am a good father."

"This is a pleasant fiction," Lucilla said with the same gentle sarcasm as they walked a ways out into the chill night air.

She understood him. She knew well that, much as Marcus Aurelius would love to be just a simple old man sharing some quiet moments with a compassionate and loving daughter, things were infinitely more complicated—and always had been. When you were the aging Emperor of the greatest power on earth, no relationships were simple, no moments were pure in the way you might wish.

NINE

In the crisp cold morning at the edge of the forest, slants of winter sunlight pierced the mist that lingered between the trees. Here, on the edge of the great army encampment, a group of men performed a strange, intense, daily ritual.

Commodus, stripped almost naked, his chiseled body covered in a fine sheen of sweat, wielded a double-weight, strength-building *gladius*, making the precise moves he would use in battle. He and his six praetorian body guards were going through their daily regimen, undergoing the same rigorous training that every legionary recruit followed. It was training taken straight from the gladiator schools, where men learned to fight for their lives.

Defying the sub-zero temperatures, Commodus and his men hacked at small trees with swords. In the rising mist and shafts of dirty sunlight, it was like an eerie, meditative workout. Commodus's concentration was so intense as to be unnerving if his men hadn't been used to it.

The young royal was proud of being fit and muscular, exceedingly so. He made a point of equaling the standard legionary training, and then going beyond it. When every month recruits had to make three eighteen-mile route marches carrying sixty-pound packs, Commodus made three twenty-four-mile

marches, each in one day, and built camp in the eve-
-ning. Recruits had to perform feats of running, tree
felling, jumping, and negotiating an obstacle course in
full armor with heavy weapons. Commodus made himself do two such drills for each one a recruit had to
do. His strength and fitness fixation was said to be
tied to his fascination with gladiators. His oft-ex-
pressed desire, which raised horrified reactions from
friends and relatives, was to enter the arena and prove
himself in combat against real gladiators. It was not a
thing a high-born Roman would ever deign to do. He
knew it would be futile to think his father might ever
give the notion his approval. His father had put an
end to the tradition of gladiator fights in Rome.

Maximus passed by the early morning training
ground, striding fast. He briefly glanced at the glisten-
ing bodies, not surprised to note the Emperor's son
among them. Then he moved on. He had heard the
stories about Commodus's obsession with physical
strength and prowess. And he had also heard rumors
about Commodus's cruel and lecherous habits—vicious assaults he was supposed to have made on slaves
and freewomen in his employ. Maximus reserved judgment on such rumors; the Imperial family was inevita-
bly a magnet for jealousy and backbiting.

Maximus approached a large network of tents, surrounded by praetorian officers. They nodded him
through the entrance. He was expected.

TEN

Maximus entered the Emperor's tent, silhouetted against the bright square of morning behind him. As the guards let the flaps fall back down, darkness returned to Marcus's chamber. Flickering oil braziers provided the only light in the enormous, luxurious Imperial tent. Heavy beams supported the canopy and creaked like the timbers of a ship as the tent swayed slightly in the wind. Marble busts of eminent Romans and Greeks on pedestals encircled the tent, set off against a rich backdrop of crimson and gold drapes, Oriental carpets, enormous bronze lamps, and silver candelabras.

Marcus sat with his back to Maximus, absorbed in writing in his journal with a quill. Looking down on him from behind his writing table was a blank-eyed bust of Homer.

"Caesar. You sent for me," Maximus said as he bowed.

Marcus, lost in his meditations, didn't respond.

"Caesar?" Maximus repeated.

"Tell me again, Maximus," Marcus said, "why are we here?"

"For the glory of the Empire, sire," Maximus replied.

Marcus seemed not to hear him. Then rising from his desk, he muttered, "Yes, I remember . . ." He walked over to a large map of the Roman Empire mounted on a frame. He waved a hand across his vast dominion. "Do you see it, Maximus? This is the world I have made. For twenty years I have written philosophy and ruminated on 'great issues.' For twenty years I have tried to cast an image of myself as the scholar and theorist . . . but what have I really done?" He touched the map—the Danubian provinces, Dacia, the East. "For twenty years I have conquered. I have spilled blood and defended the Empire. Since I became Caesar, I have only had *four years* of peace in twenty. Is that the legacy of a philosopher? And for what?" The old man shook his head in dismay.

"To secure our borders, sire," Maximus countered. "To bring civilization. Justice. Teaching."

"I brought the sword! Nothing more!" Marcus spat. "And while I've been fighting, Rome has grown diseased and corpulent. I did this. And no amount of philosophy or meditations can change the fact that Rome is far away, and we shouldn't *be* here." He turned fiercely to his listener.

"But Caesar—" Maximus started.

"Don't call me that," Marcus interrupted. "We have to talk together now. Very simply. Just as men. Can we do that?" Marcus's steady gaze challenged Maximus to respond with his own truth.

"Forty thousand of my men are out there freezing in the mud," Maximus said. "Eight thousand are cleaved and bloodied. Two thousand will never leave this place. I won't believe they fought and died for nothing."

"What would you believe, Maximus?" Marcus asked.

"That they fought for you—and for Rome," Maximus replied.

"And what is Rome, Maximus? Tell me."

"I have seen too much of the rest of the world . . . and it's brutal and cruel and dark. I have to believe Rome is the light."

Marcus nodded. Yes, this was just what he was probing for. "And yet," he said, "you've never been there. You've not seen what it's become." He seemed to retreat into his reflections once more.

Maximus only knew what he had heard: that while the Emperor had devoted years, millions of sesterces, and all his energies to quelling the barbarian storm at the Empire's frontiers, corruption had crept into every crevice at home like a pestilence. Masses of people in the cities were ill fed and food prices were astronomical, with most of the grain and corn from the provinces going straight into the storehouses of the rich. And as most of the tax and tribute money ended up in the pockets of a powerful few, the roads, bridges, and harbors of Italy—and hence the economy—were hopelessly crumbling. The famously hardworking, thrifty, civic-minded Roman people were now said to be cynical, demoralized and poor. An empire so big, so incredibly expensive to operate and defend, couldn't endure with a shamelessly corrupt ruling elite and a plummeting economy. Something had to give.

"I am dying, Maximus," Marcus said. "And when a man sees his end, he wants to know that there was some purpose to his life." He sat down to gather his strength. "It's strange," he said. "I find myself thinking little of the waning moments around me. Instead, I think of the future. I wonder . . . how will the world speak my name in years to come? Will I be known as the philosopher? The warrior? The tyrant? Or will I be the Emperor who gave Rome back her true self?"

Maximus studied the old man, his imperious hawk's eyes gleaming out of his regal, bone-thin face.

"You see—there was a dream that was Rome," Marcus said. "I can only whisper of it now. Anything more than a whisper and the dream vanishes. It's so . . . fragile. And I fear it will not survive the winter." Shakily, he held out a hand to Maximus.

Maximus took his hand, deeply moved by the Emperor's sentiment, and knelt before him.

"Let's just whisper here, you and I," Marcus said. "You have a son. You must love him very much."

Maximus bowed his head in silent assent.

"Tell me about your home," the old man said.

As Maximus began to tell him, memories of peaceful, gentler times softened the voice of the hardened warrior. "The house is in the hills above Trujillo," he said. "It is a simple place, pink stones that warm in the sun. There's a wall, a gate, a kitchen garden that smells of herbs in the day and jasmine in the evenings." He looked up. The old man had closed his eyes as he listened. He was smiling; he was there in his mind.

Maximus went on: "Through the gate is a giant cypress, with fig, apple, and pear trees. The soil, Marcus, it's black . . . black like my wife's hair. We grow grapes on the south slopes and olives on the north. Wild ponies play near the house and tease my son. He wants to be one of them."

"How long since you were last home?" Marcus said.

"Two years, two hundred sixty-four days—and one morning," Maximus said.

Marcus laughed. "I envy you, Maximus. It's good, your home." He nodded his head thoughtfully. "Worth fighting for."

He looked at Maximus much more deliberately now. From the expression in Marcus's eyes, Maximus could see that a plan seemed to be unfolding in his mind. "I have one more duty to ask of you, Maximus," he said. "Before you go home."

"What would you have me do, Caesar?" Maximus said.

"Before I die," Marcus said, "I will give the people this final gift. An empire at peace should not be ruled by one man. I mean to give power back to the Senate."

Maximus was astounded. The senatorial republican form of government had failed definitively two centuries before, and the infighting and corruption infecting the senatorial class had been no small part of it. "Sire—if no *one* man holds power," Maximus said, "all men will reach for it."

"You're right, of course," Marcus said. "That is why I ask you to become the Protector of Rome. I empower you to one end alone: to give power back to the people of Rome, and end the corruption that has crippled her."

Maximus said nothing for a long moment. It *was* a dream. To restore the noble system of government of law, political freedom, and civic responsibility that had worked so well for early Rome, the tiny city-state of ten thousand, before it grew to be the heart of an Empire that ruled the world. Rome had changed too much to return to that visionary republic.

"You don't want this great honor I offer you?" Marcus asked incredulously.

Maximus could feel a weight descending on him like nothing he had ever experienced, a responsibility that seemed even greater than commanding the entire 186,000-man, fourteen-Legion Army of the North. "With all my heart, no," he replied.

"That is why it must be you," Marcus said simply.

"Why not a senator or a prefect?" Maximus said. "Someone who knows Rome and understands her politics."

"Because you haven't been corrupted by her politics," Marcus said.

"And what about Commodus?" Maximus said.

"Commodus is not a moral man," Marcus said. "You've known that since you were young. He is not fit to rule." His eyes looked off into the distance, as though contemplating the horror of a Commodus Empirium. "He *must not rule*."

He returned his gaze to Maximus and said, "You're the son I should have had . . . although I fear that if you had truly been my son, my blood would have polluted you as it did Commodus. Our family has lived so long with power and depravity that we no longer even remember a life without it." He stood up and said matter-of-factly, "Commodus will accept my decision. He knows you command the loyalty of the army."

A sliver of ice stabbed at Maximus's heart. Though the old man meant well for both his family and his Empire, his idealism was always steadfastly rooted in the granite of real politics. "I need some time, sire," he said.

"Yes. By sunset, I hope you will have agreed," Marcus said. "Now let me embrace you as a son."

Marcus held Maximus for a long time in his grasp, as though not counting on the future to present any more such opportunities.

"Now bring an old man another blanket," Marcus said when he finally released Maximus and stepped back.

Maximus got Marcus another quilt, which the old Emperor wrapped around his thin shoulders. "We fight the winter as best we can, eh?" he said with a bleak smile.

As deep feelings stirred with his breast, Maximus bowed and left, leaving the diminished man bundled against the night's frigid chill.

ELEVEN

Maximus emerged from Marcus's tent, so stunned that he almost stumbled in front of a troop of cantering praetorian cavalry. He moved quickly to the edge of the compound. When he thought he was out of sight, he leaned an arm against a post to steady himself, trying to control his churning emotions. He stood there a long moment in the lee of the Imperial tents in the white light of morning, head down, racked with conflicted feelings.

"My father favors you now," a voice behind him said.

Maximus turned. Standing before him was Annia Lucilla, radiant in her fine Imperial cloak of snowy ermine and rich purple silk. As their eyes met, a charge of emotion sparked through them both—and both vied to conceal it.

In the background, at a discreet distance, stood a lady-in-waiting.

Maximus bowed to Lucilla. "My lady," he greeted her.

"It was not always so," Lucilla said with a half smile. The dark auburn ringlets of her hair, pulled back by a bejeweled headband, set off a face of striking and delicate loveliness.

Maximus looked at her, shaking his head slightly in

wonder. "Many things have changed since we last met," he said.

"Many things," Lucilla echoed, looking into his melancholy dark eyes. "But everything."

Maximus looked at her intently, as though marking her face and the moment in memory, then bowed slightly and turned to walk away.

"Maximus! Stop," Lucilla implored. "Let me see your face."

When he stopped, she approached him and raised a hand. "You're upset," she said.

"I've lost too many men," Maximus said quickly, dismissively.

Lucilla didn't buy his answer. Her style always was to cut through subterfuge. "What did my father want with you?" she asked.

"To wish me well, before I leave for Spain," Maximus replied.

"You're lying," Lucilla said matter-of-factly. "I could always tell when you were lying. You were never good at it."

"I never acquired your comfort with it," Maximus said with more than a trace of irony.

"True, but then you never had to," Lucilla said. "Life is simpler for a soldier . . . or do you think me heartless?" She smiled at him.

I think you are truly your father's daughter, with a hard-nosed, realistic grasp of circumstance, Maximus said to himself. Aloud, he said, "I think you have a talent for survival."

She didn't deny what he said, neither was she ashamed of it.

Maximus turned to walk away again.

"Maximus, please," she said, moving after him.

He stopped.

"Is it really so terrible seeing me again?" she said

with undisguised feeling. Color rose in her soft peach cheeks.

"No. I'm sorry," he said. "I'm tired from battle."

"And it hurts you to see my father so fragile," she said. She knew Maximus, knew his heart. They had a history, of which she had forgotten not a moment.

"Commodus expects that my father will announce his succession within days," she said. "Will you serve my brother as you served his father?"

"I will always serve Rome," Maximus said, not forgetting for an instant that he was talking to a member of the royal family, and that his loyalty was expected to be impeccable.

"Do you know I still remember you in my prayers?" Lucilla said. "Oh yes, I still pray!"

"I was sorry to hear of your husband's death," Maximus said earnestly. "I mourned him."

"Thank you," Lucilla said. Such a small, formal exchange to cover so much of life, so many complicated experiences and feelings.

"I hear you have a son," Maximus said.

"Yes," she said brightly. "Lucius. He's nearly eight years old."

"I, too, have a son who is eight years old," he replied. They smiled at each other. It was a moment in which much could have been said, many doors reopened. But those doors remained closed tight. They were on paths that could only diverge again, as they had so abruptly and irreversibly in the past.

"I thank you for your prayers," Maximus said. He gave her a warm, swift smile and left.

She watched him walk away. She crossed her hands on her breast as if to hold in the confusion of emotion that swirled inside her for this man who had once meant so much to her, whom she had once held so close.

TWELVE

Maximus knelt before his campaign table in his
tent in the near dark. He faced his ancestors, a
group of small carved figurines surrounded by candles.
Several of them represented his parents and grandpar-
ents, but there too, the smallest of the figures, surrounded and protected by the others, were a woman
and child.

"Ancestors, I ask you for your guidance," he
prayed. "Blessed mother, come to me with the Gods'
desire for my future. Blessed father, watch over my
wife and son with a ready sword." As he named them,
he touched the figurines. "Whisper to them that I live
only to hold them again, for all else is dust and air.
Ancestors, I honor you and will try to live with the
dignity that you have taught me."

Looking upon his family figures for a long reflective
moment, he tried to conjure up what his father or his
grandfather would do faced with his circumstance. It
was an extraordinary request that Marcus Aurelius
had made of him. Would they counsel him that civic
duty bade him submit to the yoke Marcus envisioned
for him to wear? Or would they murmur hubris for
his even considering he was equal to the task?

His ancestors remained silent on the question. He
sighed with a deep apprehensiveness. He picked up
the figure of his wife and kissed it, lost in his thoughts.

"Cicero," he called out.

Behind him, his manservant Cicero appeared, noiseless and discreet, and handed him a drink. "Sir?"

"Do you ever find it hard to perform your duty?" Maximus said.

Cicero was a tall, slim man with long hair and a sensitive face that was cut from ear to nose with a deep scar. "Sometimes I do what I want to do, sir," he said. "The rest of the time I do what I have to do."

Maximus smiled and nodded at the homely truth of it. "We may not be able to go home after all," he said with great regret.

"Sir?" Cicero said, a puzzled look on his face.

THIRTEEN

Marcus Aurelius, in his great tent lit only by fire-light, stood in silent contemplation of the figures of his own ancestors, preparing himself to say what he must utter. There did not seem to be the words for it, even in the vast lexicon of this gifted man of letters. Finally, he said, "You will do your duty, for Rome."

Commodus stood before him, proud and erect, ready for bestowed glory. "Yes, Father," the son said.

"But you will not be Emperor," Marcus said.

Commodus froze as he heard this. It was a thunder-bolt—a death blow to his ambitions. Nonetheless he managed to control his expression, even as his mind tumbled and sought to right itself. He gave a hint of a bow, as if accepting his father's judgment. "Which wiser, older man is to take my place?" he said with great effort.

"My powers will pass on to Maximus," Marcus said, "to hold in trust until the Senate is ready to rule once more. Rome is to be a republic again."

Though Commodus's face set into a frigid mask, he felt himself flush all over. *The old man has lost his mind!* he thought. *He has cracked up entirely.* But only the tears of rage rising in his eyes revealed anything of his feelings. "Maximus . . . ," he said quietly.

"My decision disappoints you," Marcus said. He had once had great hopes for his handsome boy: mentally acute and energetic as a student, ambitious and enterprising, full of boyish charm and enthusiasm. With the years of Imperial privilege, he had risen in rank and ability, but also in arrogance and self-absorption. He did not seem to care a fig for anyone besides himself, much less the people of Rome. Marcus Aurelius, the philosopher-king whose first thought in the morning and last thought at night was for the Empire that he served, could not place the public trust in the hands of such a man, his son or not.

Commodus stared at his father, his mind racing through possible options, shaping his response. "You wrote to me once, listing the four chief virtues," he said, temporizing. "Wisdom, justice, fortitude, temperance. As I read the list, I knew I had none of them. But I have other virtues, Father. Like ambition. That can be a virtue when it drives us to excel. Resourcefulness. Courage. Perhaps not on the battlefield, but there are many forms of courage. And devotion. To my family, and to you. But none of my virtues were on your list. Even then, it was as if you didn't want me for your son."

"Commodus, you go too far," Marcus said, deeply saddened.

"And you break my heart," Commodus said. "I search the faces of the Gods for ways to please you, to make you proud . . . yet I can never do it. One kind word, one full hug where you pressed me to your chest and held me tight would have been like the sun on my heart for a thousand years. What is it in me that you hate so much? My eyes are your eyes. My hands are your hands. All I have ever wanted was to live up to you. Caesar. *Father*." The young man could not control his tears.

Marcus, much moved, knelt down before his son.

"Commodus, your faults as a son is my failure as a father," Marcus said.

Commodus entered his father's embrace, kissing the top of his head, weeping freely. As he held his father's head, a cold light glinted in his teary eyes. "Why does Maximus deserve what I could never have?" he said with fervor. "Why do you love his eyes over mine? I would butcher the whole world . . . if you would only love me . . ." His voice grew louder as he pressed his father's face tight against his chest and held him there. Marcus began to struggle, but Commodus held his head in an iron grip, slowly suffocating him, the tears still rolling down his cheeks. The old man was no match for his youthful, muscular offspring. Commodus didn't relax his hold until he felt Marcus's body drop limp in his arms.

He laid him down on the bed, dead. "You should have loved me more," he said softly.

FOURTEEN

Maximus had turned in his bed for what seemed like half the night, pushed and pulled by the agonizing choices he would have to make once the new day lifted. Finally, he fell into a deep sleep, exhausted from battle and inner turmoil.

Yet Quintus had only to touch his shoulder. "General Maximus," he whispered, and Maximus snapped awake, swiftly placing a knife at Quintus's throat.

"Quintus?" Maximus said, his heart pounding. As he removed the blade from the man's neck, Maximus knew there was trouble—Quintus would not be awakening him in the dark for any small reason.

"The Emperor needs you," Quintus said. "It's urgent."

Maximus leapt up and threw on a cloak, then strode out into the dead of night with his number-two officer.

They moved quickly through the eerily quiet, sleeping camp. Only the watch fires on the far periphery and some intermittently barking dogs gave any sign of this small city slumbering at the edge of the pine forest.

"What is it?" Maximus said.

"I was not told," Quintus said.

Maximus quickened his pace as they approached Marcus's complex of tents. Foreboding filled his chest, making his breath shorten.

At the entrance to the Emperor's grand tent, the praetorian night guards pulled the flaps aside and allowed the commander and Quintus through.

As the two men strode into the dimly lit tent, Maximus slammed to a halt. Commodus stood before him, his white face a blank slate. Lucilla stood in a corner of the tent, her head bowed down.

But Maximus barely saw them, stunned by the sight of Marcus Aurelius lying on his bed in the composed posture of death. Maximus stared at the great man, speechless.

"Lament with me, brother," Commodus said. "Our great father is dead."

"How did he die?" Maximus said, not taking his eyes off the still form of the man he had served and loved as a friend.

"The surgeons say there was no pain," Commodus said. "His breath gave out as he slept."

Maximus glanced at Lucilla. She avoided his eyes. Maximus crossed to the bed, ignoring Commodus. He knelt there, and gently kissed the elegant old man's forehead, a ritual farewell. "How will the world speak your name now, old man?" Maximus said softly.

He then rose, and turned slowly to look at Commodus.

Commodus looked back at him levelly. After a moment, he held out his hand. "Your Emperor asks for your loyalty," he said. "Take my hand, Maximus."

Maximus had not an iota of doubt what had transpired. He ignored the outstretched hand, looking long and unblinking into the eyes of a patricidal son.

Commodus looked back just as hard, his lips set in a thin, arrogant line, confident and commanding the moment. "I only offer it once," he said.

Maximus sidestepped him and strode out of the Imperial tent without looking back. He could not bear to breathe the same air as the venal worm who bore the royal name.

Commodus nodded to Quintus.

Quintus, armed with specific, sinister instructions, left the tent.

Commodus then turned his cold gaze on Lucilla.

She crossed to the bed, and just as Maximus had, knelt and kissed her dead father on the forehead. She stayed there a moment, her head bent, offering her father her own silent promises before saying good-bye.

Then she rose and stood before her brother. Their eyes met. She slapped his face hard, twice. He recoiled, stunned. She held his surprised eyes for a moment. Then she reached down and took his right hand. She slowly raised it to her lips and kissed it.

"Hail, Caesar," Lucilla said without emotion.

FIFTEEN

Maximus dressed quickly in the lantern light of his tent. He called in Cicero. "I must talk to the senators," he said. "Wake Gaius! Wake Falco! I need their counsel."

Quintus, entering the tent just as Cicero moved to do Maximus's bidding, grabbed the manservant's arm, staying him. "Maximus—please be careful," Quintus warned. "This is not prudent—"

"*Prudent?*" Maximus spat. "The Emperor was murdered!"

"The Emperor," Quintus said steadily, "died of natural causes."

Maximus straightened up, noticing that Quintus had his dagger in his belt, his short sword in his hand. "Why are you armed, Quintus?" asked Maximus. Just as he said the words he looked toward the entrance as four Praetorian Guards, designated assassins just moments before, entered. The guards moved immediately to bind Maximus's hands and arms, their swords quickly at his throat.

"Please don't fight, Maximus," Quintus said, seeming greatly pained at this turn of events.

"Quintus—" Maximus warned.

"I'm sorry," Quintus said, a cold finality in his voice. "Caesar has spoken." Yet his eyes seemed to plead, *This is above my level. Don't ask me to defend it.*

Maximus stared at Quintus, understanding. The man owed loyalty by oath and force of law to the Imperium, to whomever occupied the throne. "Quintus . . . look at me," Maximus said. "Promise me you'll take care of my family."

"Your family will greet you in the afterlife," Quintus said quietly.

Maximus lunged at him in an explosion of fury. The praetorians quickly grabbed for the general, the one standing behind sending the flat of his sword crashing down on the prisoner's head. Maximus crumbled.

"Caesar has spoken," Quintus said again to himself, as though to reassure himself that was all the justification that was needed. "Take him as far as the sunrise and then kill him," he said to the lead Praetorian Guard.

Quintus then sheathed his sword, turned on his heel, and left.

SIXTEEN

The approach of dawn lit the forest road with light the color of lead. Fog still shrouded the trees as the five horses trotted at a steady pace along the Roman road, deeper into the province of Upper Germany, toward wilderness absolute. They had passed neither fellow traveler nor human dwelling for several hours.

The four mounted *praetoriani* led Maximus, his hands tied in front of him, his body slumped in his saddle, on his horse along the endless stone highway. Followed far enough, the formidable road would eventually lead to another frontier garrison outpost manned by the Legions. But here there was nothing— no possible ally, no hope. Maximus rolled listlessly in the saddle, betrayed and seemingly drained of energy.

"All right, this is far enough," announced Cornelius, the praetorian squad leader, a lean, tight-lipped man in his thirties. All three of his lieutenants were substantially younger.

"You two," Cornelius indicated two of the young *praetoriani.* "Take him down there where no one will find him."

The two men climbed from their horses, and Rufinus, with some effort, wrestled his sword from its sheath. Together they pulled Maximus from his horse.

Cornelius gestured to the remaining guard, Salvius,

to tend to the bridles of the other men's horses. The squad leader himself dug in his saddlebag for something to eat. He would carry out his superior's command without qualm, but felt distaste for the need to actually to see a fellow Roman citizen's blood shed.

Aponius and Rufinus dragged Maximus down a densely forested hill flanking the road. Maximus's hands were still bound in front of him. He seemed totally resigned, lacking any resistance.

But Maximus was watching his captors like a panther spies on its prey, watching their every move and manner as they trooped down the hill through the pine needles, away from the road. They were youthful, he noted, both of them. And garbed in sparkling armor— the armor of men who had never seen real battle. They were no doubt well-trained *praetoriani,* but the *praetoriani* were the Emperor's elite civil guard, effectively the private city army of the royal family and the ruling class. They almost never left Rome, and they had never tasted war, unless it was a civil war, of which there had been none in a century.

"This is good enough," Aponius said as the hill flattened out and they came into a small clearing. "Kneel."

Maximus stood and looked listlessly from man to man. He sighed as Rufinus, the tall, boyish-faced sword-wielder, moved around for a decapitating blow. Maximus turned and followed him steadily with his eyes. He drew himself up finally and said in sharp tones to the young man: "Give me a *clean* death, a soldier's death, so I can face my ancestors with dignity."

Maximus hoped the young guard would respond to that as a general's command, and that he would be preoccupied about his killing technique and his sword stroke. As a Roman, the young man would know tradition and law: A high-ranking Roman citizen like Maximus could not be executed other than honorably, and only by sword. Though he was prepared to behead the general, Maximus had asked a fellow soldier for a more dignified end.

Aponius, a thick, broad-shouldered, handsome young officer with an erect military posture, assumed a hard mien, and growled to Maximus mercilessly, "Kneel!" He placed his hand on his sword handle in warning.

Obviously uncomfortable with the situation, Rufinus looked at the still-standing Maximus. Lamely, he nodded for the prisoner to get down.

Maximus complied, and sunk to his knees to meet his doom. But his toes were curled against the ground, his whole body secretly coiling.

Rufinus positioned himself behind him. Aponius stood across from the condemned man, hand still on his sword hilt.

Maximus closed his eyes in prayer.

Rufinus raised his sword, not for decapitation, but with the point just above the nape of Maximus's neck, preparing to drive it down into his spine with both hands using his full body weight, a military execution.

Maximus instantly spun, grabbed the blade of the sword with his strong hands, and yanked it from the startled guard. Exploding to his feet, his bleeding hands gripping the sword by its cutting edges, he wheeled and swung the weapon with brutal efficiency, breaking Aponius's jaw with the hilt. In a sweeping continuation of the same move, he recoiled at blinding speed and drove the sword backward into the chest of Rufinus like a dagger, before the young guard even saw it coming. Yanking the blade free, Maximus then spun the sword in the air, catching it by the hilt and facing the reeling Aponius, fully armed.

Aponius was frantically, impotently trying to pull his sword from its scabbard.

"Frost sometimes makes it stick," Maximus said wryly.

Then he struck.

SEVENTEEN

On the road above, the other two praetorians were waiting on their horses, happy not to have to witness the bloody deed. They turned as they heard a quick yelp from below. They craned their necks, but heard nothing else.

Cornelius nodded for Salvius to check on the execution. Salvius cantered off the road and down the hill.

As he threaded his mount down through the trees in the direction from which he'd heard the sound, he peered ahead and saw nothing of his comrades. He was about to call out when he sensed movement behind him. He spun around—but was too late. He had time only to see something whirling through the air, a sword pinwheeling toward him. Transfixed in the fraction of a second he had left, he watched the blade flash toward him end over end and bury itself in his chest. He toppled with no more than a groan and landed softly on the frosty, needle-covered ground.

Cornelius was on his horse, eating his bread and sausage. When he heard a commotion below, he wrenched his horse around several times trying to look back into the trees.

With barely a sound, Maximus burst onto the road behind him. He stood facing the officer, armed with a heavy cavalry sword. "Praetorian!" he shouted.

Cornelius spun. Unsheathing his saber, he spurred

his horse and galloped toward Maximus at full speed. Maximus crouched and prepared to launch himself at the onrushing guard . . . and at the last second stepped across the path of the charging horse, throwing off Cornelius's aim. The guard and Maximus swirled together for an instant, both slashing simultaneously. Maximus struck upward and back as the horseman went by him.

Cornelius continued to gallop on past. He swayed, and looked down in disbelief. A huge gash had opened in his torso, his kidneys sliced clean through. He fell off his horse, and lay down to die.

Maximus staggered. He had also been wounded, sustaining a deep slash on his shoulder. He fought the searing pain as he moved toward the horses.

EIGHTEEN

Maximus galloped hard through the forested German wilderness on the praetorian lieutenant's horse, leading one of the other guards' horses behind him. He had wrapped the gash in his shoulder, but it was bleeding through the crude dressing. He could not afford to stop to tend to it.

As the midday sun tilted toward the west, he crossed the open plains into the eastern precincts of Gallia. Maximus pushed his mount with an urgency he had never felt before, desperately trying to reach his destination before it was too late.

Into the night, Maximus pushed the second horse to its limit, not stopping for water, food, or rest. He was in Narbonensis now, a long-Romanized part of Gaul, with breathtaking coastal mountain landscapes along the verge of the azure Mediterranean Sea. He saw nothing of what he passed, remembered nothing— he was conscious only of his heading and the agonizing amount of time that was quickly passing.

Galloping up a hill, he passed into the rugged Iberian province of Tarraconensis. He was exhausted and overheated, and he discarded his weighty armor in favor of just his rough reddish brown soldier's tunic. The horse he was on was spent as well, foam coating its neck. It was nearing collapse and would not make it to the crest of the long hill. Maximus dismounted and immediately leapt onto the remaining horse, and continued spurring it over the hill and on toward Barcino and Valentia and the hills above distant Trujillo.

In the light of early day, the mist-shrouded Spanish hills surrounding the handsome, sprawling farm villa and outbuildings were beautiful beyond measure. Away into the distance as far as eyes could see, verdant farmlands and vineyards adorned the gently rolling slopes.

An eight-year-old boy with dark reddish curly hair worked in the paddock beside the pink-stoned villa, diligently training a wild white pony on a lunge line. A comely, raven-haired woman watched her son work and smiled. The boy would have a fine riding pony by the time his father returned.

The boy stopped—he saw something. Over a hill, he could just glimpse a battle flag approaching. He screamed with joy, dropped the bridle, and ran out of the paddock. He sprinted down the lane and up the hill in the direction of the flag, calling, "Father! Father!"

The woman, too, looked toward the flag. But something about it troubled her, and an uneasy sense gripped her throat.

Her son continued to race along the road. Soon, soldiers appeared over the hill. But they were not Roman legionaries at all. The boy slowed, then stopped, confused. Twenty praetorians cantered down the road. His father was not among these strange men. He searched their faces again, looking for his father, hoping.

Behind him, his mother started yelling out his name.

The column of horses broke into a gallop and ran the small boy over, trampling him into the dirt, heading directly toward the screaming mother. . . .

NINETEEN

As the hills around the vineyards turned violet and gold with the sunset, a mounted rider raced for his life, killing the horse under him. His shoulder bled profusely, coating his leg and the flank of the horse. He galloped in a frenzy up a long gradual slope. Cresting the hill, he saw the sky over the distant ridgeline, and pulled hard on the reins, rearing the horse to a stop. He measured frantically with his eye, gauging the origins of an ominous column of thick black smoke that rose from the landscape.

With a groan of anguish escaping his lips, he spurred the horse forward, racing down the far side of the hill at a speed he prayed would outdistance the terror in his heart.

Maximus's worst nightmare did not equal what lay in front of him. His family home and farm lay smoldering, destroyed. The earth and the vineyards and the orchards were scorched black, and smoke still curled up from the scant remains of his house. Two pink-stone chimneys jutted up out of the charred debris.

He pulled up so hard on his speeding horse when they neared the house that the horse fell sideways onto the turf, trapping one of Maximus's legs. He pulled himself out from under the animal and staggered up to the smoking remnants of his house, sick with fear at what he might find—at what he knew he would find.

He spotted the incinerated bodies of servants scattered about in the ruins, and continued on, his wound bleeding more with every tortured step. He finally stopped before an arbor leading to the kitchen garden. He stared up and, as he gasped to force breath into his lungs, his knees buckled. His wife and his son had been crucified and immolated. They were nothing more than grotesquely twisted, blackened, barely human shapes. He reached up with both hands to touch what were once the feet of his wife. A horrible keening howl rose from his guts as he screamed in unearthly torment. In utter despair, he coated his face in the ashes of his now dead world.

In the vineyard on the south slope Maximus buried his wife and son at nightfall. He dug deep graves in the black loamy soil that had nourished the grapes and olives in his fields, and the figs and pears and apples in his orchards. He patted down the mounded earth gently over their defiled, broken bodies. He was weeping, almost fainting from his wound, his hands buried in the dirt. He looked up to where the kitchen garden used to be by the house he had built with these same dirt-streaked, bloodied hands, where the herb and the jasmine his wife had planted scented the air.

He spoke to his dead loved ones through his tears.

"Lie in the shade of the white poplar, my loves. Do the meadow flowers smell sweet? Wait for me there. . . ."

He collapsed into the earth.

TWENTY

They had been drawn by the telltale acrid smell of smoke in the air, as carrion eaters by the scent of a kill. Where there was fire, there would be devastation, they knew. And where there was devastation, there would be easy pickings.

An unusual jingling sound preceded their arrival, emanating from the delicate metal anklets this tribe of Basque brigands wore around their feet. They shuffled cautiously up to the man lying dead across the two freshly made graves, and moved around him looking, poking. The chief of the scavenging nomads was a burly mountain man with a greasy black beard.

Hands touched Maximus's sandals. They were rich leather military sandals lined with strips of fur. Other hands stroked his dark red soldier's tunic, admiring the fine cloth. . . .

Suddenly Maximus groaned.

The hands stopped roaming.

A bit of quick language in an unknown tongue. A moment of watchful waiting.

The big man on the ground didn't move. The brigand chief made a signal, and the hands roughly grabbed Maximus and dragged him away.

Days and nights passed, and for Maximus it was a never-ending kaleidoscopic, feverish dream. Hellish images came to him and tormented him as he sank in and out of consciousness.

How many days he dreamed and suffered and danced close with death in the jouncing wagon he didn't know.

But now the nature of his nightmares changed.

A repulsive hyena was barking at him, jaws snapping above him. . . .

In impenetrable black, the sound of seagulls, water lapping, the creak of timbers on a foul-smelling ship. He was on a sea voyage. . . .

A large African man crouched close, breathing fetid air in Maximus's face, smiling down at him viciously. . . .

A harsh desert landscape passing by like drifting clouds . . . distant mountains . . . shouts in a strange language, suffocating air so hot it clung to his skin like pitch. . . .

A dusty crocodile writhing, bound by ropes. . . .

Maximus's eyes slowly opened. Inches away from his face, looking straight down at him, a hyena snarled—one that didn't go away when he closed his eyes and opened them again. Maximus lurched back.

He looked around to realize he was in a filthy closed wagon with other men, rough sorts of several different races chained together at the ankles. Bars lined the small windows front and rear and on both sides. He was in a slave wagon. The hyena paced in a cage suspended over him.

Maximus turned to see past the hyena cage and through one of the barred windows. He could make out three other wagons moving slowly with them over the desert landscape. He thought he saw a whole menagerie of exotic animals caged in pens—leopards, lions, panthers, and bears. Slogging alongside on chains were zebras, a spotted giraffe, even a wildebeast. Maximus went light-headed and, rolling over on the floor of the wagon, passed out thinking: *This must all be just a dream. . . .*

A dozen slaves were chained together alongside sacks of spices and other cargo, looking across at him impassively. Bedouin slave traders outside the wagon jabbered in a surreal babel of foreign tongues. Someone was looking down at him, Maximus realized. A striking and muscular African with a shaved head and expressionless eyes was gazing at him, chewing something.

"Juba," said the African, giving his name. He, too, was chained.

Maximus, moving in great pain, saw that the gaping sword wound on his shoulder was teeming with large fat yellow maggots. Repulsed, he struggled to scrape them off his wound, but Juba stopped him.

"No—it's good," he said. "They will clean it. Wait and see."

Maximus looked at the man as if he was a lunatic, and fell back, once again lapsing into unconsciousness from the agony of his wounds.

Maximus awoke to find Juba carefully placing a paste that he had been chewing into the folds of his wound.

"Better now?" Juba said. "Clean. You see!"

Maximus hissed in pain as Juba massaged the paste gently into the gash. The massive African swept his eyes around the caravan, indicating the animals that surrounded them. "Don't die," he said. "They'll feed you to the lions. They're worth more than we are. I think we are worth more than the hyenas, though. So they don't feed us to them."

Maximus stared at him. Juba looked down at him with the barest hint of a smile.

TWENTY-ONE

The heat of Morocco was unlike anything Maximus had ever known. The air was so thick and hot and dust-choked that simply breathing was hard, even if he cared about breathing, and he didn't. He barely had the strength of will to stand in the shimmering heat waves that rippled over the sand. All around him, men of many backgrounds made a market in slaves of many races.

The provincial market was bustling like the Agora in Rome, but here the prime goods were human, with slave traders and dealers and merchants circulating around the goods, all talking very quickly and emphatically. The chained slaves on display were poked and prodded and fondled by would-be buyers. The smiling, densely black-bearded Bedouin slave trader sang out their praises to passers-by.

Maximus stood motionless among the slaves, gazing far away. He was physically recovering from his wound, but his eyes reflected the void in his heart. Deep down there was only darkness in his soul: He no longer cared for anything, not even his own life. That he stood among slaves, a slave in chains himself, made no impression on him. Maximus the husband and vineyard keeper, the general of the Army of the North, was dead. He was the walking, breathing form of a man, but his will was destroyed. He stood among the other slaves empty of any self that might demand regard or human recognition.

Across the square, Aelius Proximo sat out of the midday sun under the awning of a seedy café, watching everything like a hawk.

Proximo was a man with big, azure eyes, greasy white hair, and a jutting white beard cropped to a point, all of it giving him the ferocious appearance of a true pirate. His generous girth under his belted caftan, along with his restlessly roving gaze, suggested a man of ravenous appetites. He sipped his tea as a tradesman measured his feet for new sandals. Two slave girls squatted beside him lazily swatting at flies with switches.

"Proximo! My old friend!" the grinning Bedouin slave trader called out as he spotted the watchful pirate.

Proximo turned toward him, then turned away.

The Bedouin approached, smiling broadly. "Every day is a great day when you are here," he said to Proximo. "And today is your most fortunate day."

Proximo turned and slammed his hand into the man's groin, grabbing him there through the folds of his jelab. The slave trader opened his mouth and doubled up, leaning in to Proximo, squeaking in pain.

"Those giraffes you sold me won't mate!" Proximo said. "All they do is run around and eat! You sold me queer giraffes!"

The slave trader choked out an answer through his pain. "You're too impatient," he whined. "It's not the season. Give them time."

"Give me my money back," Proximo demanded.

"I'll give you a special price," the slave trader wheezed. "Just for you, a valued customer, a family price!"

"On what?" Proximo said.

"Have you seen the new lions?" the Bedouin said. "Come and see them!" He gestured toward his wares, urging Proximo hopefully.

Proximo released his grip and the Bedouin hobbled off toward his merchandise, nursing his bruised privates. "Adude, Ashwad!" the trader called to his servants in Berber. "Come on, Quick!"

Proximo rose and walked. His girl servants and several manservants hurried close behind him, knowing their master's every need without being told.

"This one is my beauty," the trader said, standing before a lion in a cage.

Proximo tried to goad it, and getting no response, lost interest. He walked on to another lion. "Do they fight?" he asked skeptically as he ambled around the cage.

"Of course. Like . . . lions," the slave trader said. He gave a bray of laughter.

Proximo chuckled. Then he saw the crocodiles. They interested him. He straddled one, forcing its mouth open to look inside.

"You have a good eye," the Bedouin said. "Crocodiles that size—you cannot find them anymore."

"It's just about enough for a trunk and a pair of slippers," Proximo said. "How much?"

"For you—my special price—eight thousand sesterces," the Bedouin said.

"For me, four thousand sesterces," Proximo countered. "That's for the lions too."

"Four?" the slave trader exploded. "Master, I have to eat. . . ."

Proximo cast his eyes around for more bargains, and saw the group of chained humans. "Do any of them fight?" he said. "I have a match coming up."

"Some are good for fighting," the trader said. "Some for dying. You need both."

Proximo sauntered over and eyeballed Juba. "Get up," he commanded the big African.

Juba slowly lifted his head to look at him. He got up reluctantly.

Proximo felt his flesh exactly as if he were a field animal. He turned over Juba's palms and felt the toughness of the skin. "Numidian?"

Juba nodded.

"What's your trade?" Proximo said.

"I was a hunter," Juba said.

The slave trader scoffed, shaking his head, scurrying along in Proximo's wake. "I bought him from the salt mines of Carthage," he said.

Proximo moved on to Maximus. The slave trader passed Juba, hitting him on the arm to sit down.

Proximo saw the still-festering wound in Maximus's shoulder. Flies had settled on it. Proximo pulled out a scarf and prodded the wound sharply. Maximus barely flinched. Proximo withdrew the scarf, disgusted at the pus and gore. It was then he saw a small tattoo just above the wound—the letters "SPQR."

"The mark of the legions," Proximo said with interest, *"Senatus Populusque Romanus."* He knew well what that stood for: The Senate and Roman People. It was an ancient motto reminding legionaries for whom they worked and fought. "You a deserter?" he said, eyeing the impassive big man.

Maximus said nothing.

"Probably," said the eager slave trader. "Who cares? He's a Spaniard, they say."

Proximo moved on to check out the others. "I'll take six, a thousand for the lot," he said. He held out one hand, not looking. His servant was ready: He placed in Proximo's hand a small brush loaded with red pigment from a small pot.

"A thousand!" the Bedouin exclaimed. "The Numidian alone is worth two thousand." He murmured low to Proximo, "Turn your back on him, he'll kill you."

"These slaves are rotting," Proximo said, unimpressed.

"It all adds to their flavor," the slave trader said.

Proximo walked away.

"Wait, wait . . . ," the Bedouin pleaded. "We can negotiate."

Proximo made his mark on the slaves he had picked with a daub of red paint on the chests of their rough wool tunics. "I'll give you two thousand," he said. "And four for the beasts, which makes five thousand. For an old friend."

The slave trader sighed and accepted. "For an old friend," he said.

"But the lions—they have to fight," Proximo said.

"Don't feed them for a day and a half," the Bedouin said, "and they'll eat their own mothers. Raw."

"Interesting idea," Proximo said, looking as though he actually thought it might be a workable idea. He gave a wave of one hand, and his servants grabbed the chains fastened to Maximus and Juba and the others and dragged them toward one of Proximo's slave wagons.

TWENTY-TWO

Proximo's mule-drawn caravan rumbled through the crowded casbah of a cramped, dismal Moroccan port city.

Maximus and Juba sat crammed in a wagon with a dozen other newly bought slaves, one of whom was a very scared and reedy Greek who, emitting an occasional whimper, gave the appearance of being a clerk or scribe of some sort.

The slave wagon was followed by several other wagons filled with exotic animals, including the lions. Most of the chained men glanced back at the lions, not with interest but with fear. They all knew what a hungry lion could do, and they suspected why they and the beasts had been bought in the same package.

Just outside the casbah, the caravan approached an imposing set of iron gates. Subservient attendants pulled the gates open and, bowing, let the wagons pass.

There was no sign on the gate or on the buildings inside, but everyone in the city knew the place as Proximo's School. It was not a place to learn Latin and arithmetic sums and Greek prosody. It was a school to learn how to fight and survive in order to live one more day in the face of contrived mayhem and death. It was a gladiator school.

Proximo's provincial academy resembled nothing so

much as a run-down castle prison. The fading grandeur of the decaying battlements, thick mud-brick walls, and sweeping Moorish architecture only slightly mitigated the brutal feel of the place.

The compound opened out in the center into a kind of quadrangle. On one side of the courtyard were a series of cages filled with feral animals of every description. Proximo's house slaves began unloading the newly purchased exotic beasts and running them into empty cages.

Maximus and the new slaves were next. With heavily armed guards supervising every move, house slaves grabbed their chains, getting ready to pull them toward human holding pens on the opposite side of the central quad.

A roar of commotion drew Maximus's eyes to Proximo, who, surrounded by his servants and animal handlers, was "playing" with a lion through the cage bars, taunting it with a rotting leg of mutton.

Maximus recoiled as slaves banged back the doors and prodded him and the other new men with staves, herding them out of the cages like cattle.

Maximus took in the imposing walls and the heavily armed guards. The ground-level guards had short Roman *gladius* swords hanging at their hips. Many of them wore bronze-studded leather "knuckles" on their fists. Others casually handled maces and chain whips. Guards at half a dozen points on the roof had Syrian short bows slung over their shoulders, clutches of metal-barbed arrows ready on the battlements.

At the far end of the compound, a dozen men engaged in spates of combat. A lean, muscled trainer hurled fist-sized rocks at a slighter but equally tough-looking man, who parried the stones with a small round shield. Two others took turns lunging at each other with heavy trident spears, parrying with heavy nets.

Battle practice, thought Maximus.

An immense man in a ragged coarse wool tunic and heavy leather belt instructed two new gladiators how to throw a spear. His two pupils missed the man-shaped target chalked on a board. The powerful instructor, who had the shoulders of a water buffalo, flung and hit the target right in the stomach.

"Haken," admired a voice from behind, naming the instructor.

Maximus turned to look at Proximo, who was complimenting the controlled power of Haken, one of his prize pieces of manflesh. He and Maximus locked eyes once again.

"Deserter . . . ," Proximo said, naming Maximus; then he moved down the line designating the other new slaves: "Thief . . . murderer. . . ."

Suddenly he grinned, bursting with goodwill. "Proximo!" he exclaimed. "Anyone know what that means? 'Nearest.' 'Dearest.' 'Close to.' I am Proximo. I shall be closer to you in the next days than the bitch who brought you screaming into this world. What did she give you? A few years in this miserable hellhole you call life. I will give you something that will last forever."

Slaves tossed thick handfuls of powdered lime all over the new slaves, who coughed and clenched their stinging eyes shut. The disinfecting lime coated their wet bodies, scalding away body lice and other unwanted travelers and parasites on the sojourners.

"I did not pay good money to buy *you*," Proximo said. "I paid to buy your *death*. Whether you die alone, in pairs, or in groups, who knows? Many variations, with just one ending." He walked around his new charges, relishing this occasion for eschatological musings. "Most men die shivering, stinking, and alone. They cling to life like children clinging to their mothers' skirts. But you—you will stare death in the eye! You will challenge death to take you in your prime!" He examined the faces of the new men, looking for any reaction. "And when you die—and die you shall— your transition shall be to the sound of trumpets blaring your fanfare."

Proximo raised his hands and began to clap gently, following with a short, respectful bow. "Gladiators, I salute you," he said.

TWENTY-THREE

Basic training for the new recruits was an activity Proximo would never miss. He learned so much about the new boys.

The more experienced gladiators worked out against each other with a variety of different weapons: spiked maces, long swords, five-tined tridents, staves, and spears. They worked in different matchups and combinations, and with several kinds of shields and body armor.

The novices were herded together into a central ring. One by one they were given heavy wooden swords and sent in to face the trainers, also similarily armed.

Proximo watched from a little way off, sizing up his new freshman class. Very quickly his trained eye would sort the crop into two parts. He would signal to the servant with the pigment pots and small brushes. The potential fighters would be marked with red, and the fodder with yellow.

Thick-necked, belligerent Haken, a classic bully who had found his ideal calling, took great pleasure in knocking away the swords of the newcomers and then delivering punishing blows that landed them in the dirt. A prisoner of war from the first Marcomanni-Quadi revolt on the upper Danube, he had nothing to

The great Roman general, Maximus,
turned heroic gladiator.

Emperor Marcus Aurelius, surveying the field as his loyal soldiers wage war against Germania.

General Maximus, bloodied but unbowed.

The new emperor, Commodus, confers with
Senator Gracchus.

Maximus and Lucilla, daughter of Marcus Aurelius,
share a quiet moment reminiscing about the past.

Gracchus addresses the new emperor about the state of Rome.

The lovely Lucilla.

Maximus and Juba battle fiercely side-by-side.

The ruthless Emperor Commodus stares down
a chained Maximus.

Proximo, the great trainer of gladiators.

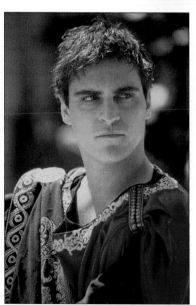

Emperor Commodus, overlooking the grand Colosseum.

The emperor and his sister enter Rome by chariot,
flanked by a grand Praetorian Guard escort.

Maximus fights for his life against the immense
gladiator Tigris.

Desperately battling Commodus, the man responsible for laying his life in ruin, Maximus exacts his revenge.

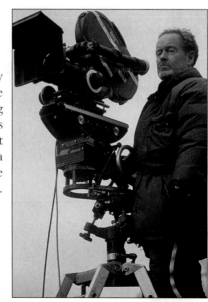

Director Ridley Scott, behind the camera, bringing the glorious battles of the ancient Roman arena back to the big screen.

lose from being constantly foul-tempered, and everything to gain.

It was soon Maximus's turn to face the powerful
instructor. "Spaniard," Haken called to him.

Maximus slowly opened his eyes, looked around,
and got up. Proximo's guards prodded him forward to
face the giant barbarian.

Proximo watched closely, to see what the former
Roman soldier would do. He had a hunch about this
man, despite the apparent lifelessness in his demeanor.

Maximus picked up the sword and stood before
Haken. And suddenly everyone was aware, Haken
most of all, that this was a man who knew how to
fight. It was something in his posture, in the way he
held the wooden weapon—but most of all, it was his
eyes. He looked at the barbarian with a steady, powerful gaze.

He raised the sword in defiance, a gesture that con-
veyed that he could kill with this sword, but chose not
to—and dropped the weapon to the ground, looking
at Haken with contempt.

Haken gave a grunt of surprise. A murmur ran
round the onlookers. Was this an insult? A mockery?

Proximo eyed the proceedings carefully, stopping in
mid-drink.

Haken looked to Proximo for instructions.

Proximo nodded.

Maximus just stood there, staring with passive eyes,
now completely unarmed.

Haken struck Maximus across the stomach. Maximus doubled up for a moment, but then stood upright
and faced him once more.

Haken looked to Proximo again, who nodded.

Haken struck Maximus heavily on his scarred arm.
Maximus staggered and almost fell, but managed to
straighten up yet again. His steady gaze bore into

Haken, enraging the instructor. Haken and everyone
else could see the challenge. I may be low, but I'm
not so low as you, Maximus was saying to him. I could
kill, but not for sport.

Proximo was fascinated. As Haken, furious, raised
his sword again, ready to do real damage, Proximo
spoke: "That's enough for the moment," he said. "His
time will come." To his servant with the pots of pigment he said, "Mark that one."

TWENTY-FOUR

In a dusty inner courtyard in the stagnant heat of late afternoon, Haken, Juba, the Greek, and other new gladiators sat on the ground in what amounted to a continuous cell—little more than a long roof with a back wall. But it was blessedly shaded.

They were playing a game with two cobras—tossing bits of gold between the venomous serpents for other players to try and snatch away. Most often the gold pebbles went unclaimed, and Haken laughed.

Maximus lay curled in a hole in the wall to one side, scraping at his shoulder with a sharp stone.

Juba called out to him: "Spaniard! Why didn't you fight? We all have to fight."

Maximus didn't answer.

The young, slightly built, bearded Greek misfit spoke from a state of terror. "I don't fight," he said. "I shouldn't be here. I'm a scribe—I can write down seven languages."

"Good," Haken said. "Tomorrow you can scream in seven languages."

The other gladiators laughed.

Juba moved closer to Maximus, looking curiously at him as he continued to rub his shoulder.

It was impossible for Maximus to hide what he had been doing as Juba settled down on the dirt beside him. He was scraping not at his scabbed wound, but at the tattoo on his shoulder, gouging off the SPQR.

"Is that the sign of your Gods?" Juba said.

Maximus didn't answer.

Over by the game, they were still taunting the poor scribe.

"Perhaps the scribe'll be the one who wins his freedom," Haken said, then cackled.

Maximus's head lifted, as though that one word had cut clear through to the core of his being. *Freedom.* The other gladiators were laughing, but the scribe took it seriously.

"Freedom!" he said. "What do I have to do?"

"You go in the arena and you kill me," Haken replied, "and him, and the Numidian, and the deserter"—he jabbed a finger at Maximus—"and a hundred more. And when there's no more to fight, you're free."

"I can't do that," the scribe said, despairing.

"No," Haken said, suddenly growing serious, "but I can." His hard gaze traveled from gladiator to gladiator and they fell silent. His eyes came to rest on Maximus.

Maximus stared steadily back at him, his face set like stone.

TWENTY-FIVE

Proximo's house slaves held a parasol over him as he made his way down a tight street in the dye market. The upper floors of houses crowded over the street, shading it with sheaves of soaking dyed wool hung to dry in the sun. Vermillion and crimson dyes dripped down and splashed across the parasol—and on the backs of the crew of gladiators following behind, staining their tunics.

Maximus, Juba, and the formidable Haken were chained to a heavy log that they carried, as were the frightened scribe and several other gladiators. Proximo's guards walked alongside them with weapons in hand.

Haken leaned forward to speak to Maximus. "The Gods favor you," he said, indicating a dark splotch of dye on his back. "Red is the Gods' color. You'll need their help today."

The terrified Greek scribe was muttering a prayer in his native tongue. Haken stared straight ahead. Juba quietly hummed a chant that seemed to transport him to another, more idyllic place.

A pack of enthralled children marched alongside them, whispering to one another about the men's physiques and fierce faces—then spitting at them, shouting out insults in their own language.

The children were not unusual, Maximus knew.

They aptly mirrored the strange double reactions that gladiators evoked wherever they went: fascination and revilement. They were brave battlers and outcasts both, heroes and criminals, the doomed and sometimes the redeemed.

Maximus watched the children for a moment and then another sight drew his attention. Over some buildings beyond, he could see vultures circling in the distance.

Provincial arenas were modest structures, inspired by the grandeur of the mighty Colosseum in Rome, but built in rough approximation only. Provincial governors, out in the colonies for career-enhancing tours of duty, built Colosseum-style arenas to entertain and Romanize the occupied peoples—and make themselves feel closer to home.

No one would mistake this shabby sand pit for the real thing. It was little more than a circle of barren ground encircled by flimsy bleachers, with thin cloth awnings strung overhead on poles. But it was filled with avid, expectant spectators all the same.

The procession of gladiators arrived in a busy, bustling street outside the arena. They passed an enclosure of prisoners and some cages holding lions, then moved on into an area piled high with dead carcasses of humans and animals. Vultures were excitedly hopping around the carcasses, preying on the meat.

In the cramped athlete holding area, a dugout beneath the arena stands, Maximus and the other gladiators milled around getting themselves armored by Proximo's guards.

Above the dugout was a railed box, where Proximo sat with several other gladiator trainers. They gossiped and postured, drank wine and ate liberally. Their vantage point, in addition to giving them a prime, head-level view of the arena, overlooked the gladiators below where preparations were going on apace.

The trainers studied the contestants, discussing their merits and making wagers. Each trainer refrained from talking about his newest, untested athletes, and at the same time belittled his known performers, trying to wheedle better betting odds.

As the trainers talked, Maximus's eyes were on the wretched group sitting huddled in the nearby prisoners' cage: old men, women, children. They looked like the refugees that fled before the victorious Roman Legions. He asked Juba who they were.

Christians, Juba told him. One of the children, a boy not much older than Maximus's son, turned and looked at him with bewildered, terrified eyes.

All around Maximus was the rattle of armor. Above him was the laughter and voices of the trainers. "Still leading with the German?" a bald, fat trainer asked.

"The crowds love a barbarian," Proximo said. "He's making me rich."

"Has the Numidian fought before?" a whiskered, yellow-toothed trainer asked.

"No. First time," Proximo replied.

"And that one?" the bald trainer said, pointing with his eyes toward the formidable figure of Maximus. "Laborer? Soldier?"

"Him?" Proximo said dismissively. "He might as well be a masseur for what he brings to the ring. In fact, that gives me an idea." He yelled out to one of his trainers: "Chain the Spaniard to the Numidian!" He turned back to his fellow trainers. "At least give the crowd the thrill of an amputation."

The fat man regarded Proximo suspiciously. He liked the looks of Maximus. "I'm not so sure," he said. "What if I wager you a thousand this Spaniard lives through the fight?"

"You're asking me to bet against my own man?" Proximo said. "I don't do that."

"Don't take me for a Thracian, Proximo," the fat man said. "What if I make it five thousand?"

A glint appeared in Proximo's eyes. That was a lot of money.

TWENTY-SIX

Waiting in a staging area, Maximus watched the little group of Christians. He knew the Christians' history, and knew that their use in these types of events was hardly new. When the city of Rome burned under Nero, the mad Emperor fingered Christians as the arsonists and contrived a grotesque punishment. He had them bound and painted with pitch, then positioned around the arena and set on fire as illumination for nighttime spectacles.

Now the Christians were forced to their feet by guards, and pushed through a door into the sun-bleached arena. At the same time, Maximus and his group were herded in the opposite direction, toward a holding cell just off the arena. Maximus stole one last glimpse of the bewildered boy before he ran off after his mother.

From the adjoining cage, Maximus glimpsed some lions as they growled and slashed at one another and slinked through an open gate into the bright sunlight of the arena.

In the holding cell, Proximo's guards lined the gladiators up in order of their planned combat. From the arena came the shrieks and agonized screams of dying Christians, barely heard over the feverish roar of the spectators as the lions did their grisly work.

The scribe was pushed to the end of the cell nearest

the barred door. He looked over and saw what awaited him and Proximo's other men: the *andabatae,* gladiators garbed as monsters from Greek and Roman myth. One was dressed as a Minotaur, half bull and half man, while others wore fearsome looking, large helmets that gave them the appearance of fierce creatures.

"Silence! Sit down!" a guard called out as he walked in.

As the gladiators sat, Proximo walked in. He waited a moment until he was sure that he held their attention.

As he did, a donkey passed by the opening to the arena, dragging the bodies of some Christians away.

"Some of you are thinking you won't fight," Proximo said, "and some that you can't fight. They all say that. Until they're out there. Listen. . . ." He cocked his head to the deafening cheers of the arena crowd. He then pulled a sword down from a shelf. "Thrust this into another man's flesh, and they will applaud and love and revere you. And you may even begin to love them back for that."

He stuck the sword point hard into a table. "Ultimately we are all dead men," he said. "Sadly, we cannot choose how. But we can decide how we accept that end, so we are remembered as men. You go out into the arena as slaves. You come back—*if* you come back—as gladiators."

The crowd outside was getting impatient.

Proximo turned to head back to his box. Before leaving, he nodded to the blacksmiths, waiting with open shackles and chains. He walked down the line, indicating who was to be chained to whom, then left to seek his seat for the show.

The blacksmiths slammed shackles on the gladiators' wrists, linking them together in teams of two by a chain four feet long. It was clear the method was to chain a "Red" to a "Yellow"—a good fighter to a certain loser.

Haken was chained to the weeping scribe. The big German tribesman never even looked down. He didn't plan to stay tethered to the wretched Greek for long.

The blacksmiths chained Maximus, a self-designated "loser" for his refusal to fight Haken earlier, to Juba.

Maximus turned his gaze to the closed door, and heard the deafening shouts of the crowd. Abruptly he knelt and scraped up a little sand from the floor, then rubbed it between his hands. Juba watched him, not understanding the ritual. When Maximus rose, his body posture was altered. He stood poised, tensed, ready for battle.

The gladiators faced a huge double door. Outside the crowd was on its feet, stamping their feet and shouting loudly.

The scribe, shaking with fear next to Haken, could barely stand. A trickling noise drew the men's attention to the floor. The scribe was pissing himself, leaving a noxious puddle on the ground around his feet.

Drums joined the thundering noise outside. Everyone stood tensed and anxious.

The doors to the arena crashed open, and sunlight burst in like an explosion, partially blinding the men for half a second. The first man out ran head-on into a huge spiked ball swung by an *andabata* who was waiting. Blood flew everywhere, and the man fell to the ground dead, his skull crushed and oozing onto the arena floor.

Side by side, their chain dangling loose between them, Maximus and Juba ran into the arena.

In the glaring tropical sun, a dozen menacing *andabatae* closed in on them. To the cheers of the crowd, they charged among Proximo's chained teams and began swinging their weapons, eager to kill.

It was a fixed fight. The *andabatae* wore huge iron helmets, tunics of chain mail, their sword arms sheathed in sleeves of forged, jointed metal. They carried swords, battle-axes, and long, heavy, five-pronged tridents, their tines filed to razor sharpness. The gladiators entered the fray bareheaded, armorless but for small round shields or none at all, wearing nothing but their scant gray tunics, carrying simple swords.

Maximus and Juba fought two *andabatae* side by side. Juba came under attack from an *andabata* wearing a menacing horned helmet and wielding both a broad-blade axe and sword. He was surprised to see out of the corner of his eye that Maximus—his partner marked with the yellow of cowards—was going after his man with focused ferocity.

The anguish and rage Maximus had buried in him welled up. After all the glories he had won in battle, after the severe losses and painful iniquities he had suffered, he knew it would not be his day to die, not like this. He slew his attacker with one blow, smashing his sword into the man's throat.

Juba knocked the sword away from his man but then lost his own weapon to a vicious swipe of the axe. The *andabata's* blade was just crashing down on Juba when Maximus pulled him clear. He blocked the axe with his shield and stabbed the man with such enormous force in the chest, that his sword point came out the man's back.

Haken fought with massive power, dragging the cowering, weeping Greek scribe with him as he went after the warrior dressed as Minotaur. He slashed at the masked figure, then gathered the scribe toward him and threw him onto the end of the Minotaur's sword. As the scribe fell to the ground screaming,

Haken drove the Minotaur back and turned to hack off the scribe's hand in order to release himself. Wielding the chain, with the scribe's hand still attached, he flailed at the Minotaur's helmet, then slashed him in the chest. As the *andabata* fell backward, Haken took advantage of his opponent's loss of balance, and savagely stabbed him to death.

Juba didn't ask how or why Maximus decided to become a fighter again. There was no time—other *andabatae* encircled the two, closing in for the kill like a pack of ravenous wolves. Back to back, Juba and Maximus made their stand, and every attacker that came near them tasted their blades. With good instinctive teamwork, ice-cold nerve, massive strength and blinding speed, they worked at evening the numbers.

Proximo watched intently.

The crowd, realizing what was going on, began to applaud and cheer the savage pair, who cut down one *andabata* after another.

Of the five other Proximo teams, one was hacking its way to victory, and another had met defeat—both gladiators lay dead, their corpses already being dragged back to the arena's perimeter. Two other teams were down to one man and losing to the onslaught of *andabatae* warriors, and both men in the last team were about to be killed, ensnared in a weighted net.

Maximus and Juba violently waylaid both of the net- and trident-wielding *andabatae* from behind with roundhouse sword blows, leaving the two gladiators to struggle free of the net's embrace.

Haken stepped in and picked up an *andabata* in another fight and impaled him on a spike at the side of the arena.

Maximus took up a dropped trident and stabbed the last *andabata* to the ground.

Juba and Maximus looked around, exhausted yet relieved, and looked at each other with the respect of fellow warriors. But just as they began to relax, they saw the last *andabata* pull the trident painfully out of his torso and start to rise. They spun and ran at the man, garotting him with the chain that joined them, sending him crashing into the wall.

Finally, the fighting was over. The *andabatae* were dead.

As Maximus surveyed the carnage around him, a strange, almost surreal sound arrested his attention. He looked up. His attention was drawn to the sound of one person clapping. Then a few more joined in, then more still, until the arena erupted in wild, un-abandoned applause. Maximus looked at the excited faces of the people, thinking that finally, he must indeed be in Hades.

He walked toward the tunnel and, in an act of utter contempt, hurled his sword into the crowd.

It only made them cheer for him more.

Proximo stood, applauding with the rest. He had lost money, but had gained a fighter. He threw his purse toward the trainer whose bet he had taken. The trainer failed to catch it and it fell to the arena sands, resting at the feet of another giant costumed figure who had just then entered the arena. This was Pluto, a crowd favorite. He moved about the ring with his sword, making sure all the bodies were dead, dispatching them with brutal thrusts of his broad sword. With their deaths, the day's brutal spectacle had ended.

TWENTY-SEVEN

It was a special day in Rome, a declared holiday.

A column of fifty stern, black-armored, helmeted Praetorian Guards came marching down the Sacra Via, the great principal parade street of Rome, leading a procession of men seated on magnificent steeds.

At the head of the mounted brigade was a chariot bearing a special personage—Commodus, son of the fallen Marcus Aurelius, heir to his father's throne. Commodus was pristinely regal in his gold-trimmed, polished parade armor, a handsome white linen cape and a gold laurel wreath crowning his head. With him rode his sister Annia Lucilla, sublimely elegant in jeweled tiara and flowing silk garments.

Another fifty praetorians marched proudly to their rear.

Close to the Imperial chariot on a black stallion rode Quintus, the new commander of the Praetorian Guards.

This was the new Emperor's ceremonial entry into Rome. Much behind-the-scenes groundwork and detailed planning had been done to get to this point. From long distance, once his father the Emperor was dead, Commodus had quickly put into effect the plans he had laid down before even leaving for the Danube front weeks before.

His lieutenants met with key senators in Rome and

reaffirmed the promises of lavish and lucrative favoritism and plum appointments that Commodus himself had made to curry their support. The now-comfortable lawmakers were also informed in plain terms that Commodus was now commander-in-chief of the entire Thirty-Legion Roman Army, and that he had the army's unswerving loyalty and support. No senator or other political figure had the power, popularity, or guts to gainsay his claim at that moment. The Senate, gnashing its teeth at their impotency, went through the rubber-stamp motions of voting and "elected" Commodus Rome's new Emperor, legitimatizing his power grab. This served to also avoid an outburst of fratricidal mayhem among pretenders, which would certainly have occurred had Marcus Aurelius's seat remained unfilled for even a matter of days.

The word had gone forth to the people. Their new Emperor—who had taken for his Imperial name Marcus Aurelius Commodus Antoninus—would arrive in the capital on this date at this time, and would make his triumphal entry to the golden city at the heart of his Empire. The city was cleaned up, and purple-hemmed bunting was draped from monuments and columns. The citizens of Rome dutifully lined the streets at the appointed hour.

It was not a vast crowd, as traditionally turned out for the Triumphs of returning victorious generals. Those were occasions to honor a military hero, ogle the spoils of war he brought back in gleaming, heaped-up plunder wagons, and marvel over the exotic animals he transported from newly conquered lands. For a true military Triumph, people turned out to celebrate the ever-growing glory of Rome and to jeer at the wagonloads of shackled prisoners of war. The crowds were invariably enthusiastic, because a Triumph meant that games at the Colosseum and huge lavish feasts and cash distributions would not be far behind. Largesse would flow from the victorious general looking to translate his popularity into political power.

The crowd for this procession was not big, nor were they particularly enthusiastic. They did manage some half-hearted cheers while they eyeballed the new young political leader with a certain jaded skepticism. It was not his lack of experience that made citizens leery—his father had arranged for him to serve terms in the series of high Roman offices that usually preceded a man's assuming the Emperorship. Instead it was his reputation as a self-absorbed, self-aggrandizing young snot that made the people think that perhaps they weren't getting the best deal here, especially in comparison to the great and good Emperor he was succeeding. Commodus would have much work to do to gain popular support if he was to hold on to his newly forged power.

Ahead in the Forum Romanum, on the grand steps of the Senate, a group of senators stood waiting to receive the luminaries: Falco, Gaius, and the formidable Senator Gracchus among them.

Lucius, Lucilla's eight-year-old son, stood with them as they watched the new Emperor's procession approach.

Senator Gracchus, a shrewd and authoritative man in his sixties, who carried himself with genuine senatorial dignity, had the ironic look of one who was only there because protocol required it. He was underwhelmed by this new young Imperial monarch. "He enters Rome like a conquering hero," Gracchus said, "but what has he conquered?"

"Give him time, Gracchus," Falco answered. "He's young. I think he could do very well."

"For Rome?" Gracchus replied. "Or for you?"

Falco turned to Lucius, who stood very straight, every inch the young prince. "A proud day for us all, eh, Lucius?" Falco said. He threw a sly look at Gracchus. "I'm sure Senator Gracchus never thought he'd live to see such a day."

"I give thanks to the Gods for my mother's safe return," Lucius said formally, his eyes on the nearing procession.

Gracchus smiled, touched by the boy's determination to be grown-up. "Go to her, Lucius," he said gently. "It's what she'd want."

The boy happily ran down the broad steps as the Emperor's procession drew to a halt before the senatorial reception. As the crowd cheered and applauded, the chariot carrying Commodus and Lucilla drew up and stopped. Lucius jumped up into his mother's arms. She hugged him tight, kissing him all over his eager cherubic face.

Commodus raised his arm in salute and looked about him at the welcoming crowd, playing the part of the triumphal ruler. But even he could see the reserved nature of the popular response.

A small child was prodded forward with a large bouquet of flowers. Commodus accepted the bouquet with a smile, patting the child on the head.

"Rome greets her new Emperor!" Falco said, descending the steps with the other senators. "Your loyal subjects bid you welcome, Highness."

Commodus tossed the bouquet of flowers aside, where it was caught by one of his entourage. "Thank you, Falco," he said. "And for bringing out the loyal subjects." He nodded at the gathered crowd with the trace of a sarcastic grin. "I trust they weren't too expensive."

Gracchus made a small, pleading bow. "Caesar."

"Ah. Gracchus," Commodus said. "The friend of Rome."

"We rejoice in your return, Caesar," Gracchus said. He suddenly grew somber. "There are many matters that require your attention."

TWENTY-EIGHT

In the marble atrium of his Imperial Palace, Commodus attempted to make nice with the delegation of senators. He knew that establishing these relationships came with the job, and that the Senate could be a valuable tool for political gain. He would do as his sister counseled him, and listen to them respectfully.

With Gaius and Falco beside him, the august, white-robed Gracchus made the Senate's presentation to the young monarch. Referring to a scroll he held open in his hands, Gracchus announced, "For your guidance, sire, the Senate has prepared a series of protocols to begin addressing the problems in the city."

Commodus, still wearing the gold laurel wreath in his hair, prowled restlessly around the room as he listened. This meeting had been going on for too long already, the doddering clowns. He grew impatient.

Lucilla sat to one side, listening intently, watching her brother with a touch of apprehension.

Showing the scroll, Gracchus went on, "Starting with basic sanitation in the Greek Quarter. We must combat the plague springing up there. If Caesar could study this—"

Commodus had had enough. "You see, Gracchus, that's the very problem, isn't it?" he interrupted. "My father spent all his time at study, poring over books of learning and philosophy. He spent his twilight hours reading scrolls from the Senate. All the while, the people were forgotten."

"The Senate *is* the people, Caesar," Gracchus said. "Chosen from among the people, to speak for the people."

Commodus could not abide being lectured to by these outdated old career politicians. "I doubt many of the people eat so well as you do, Gracchus," he said. "Or have such splendid mistresses, Gaius. I think I understand my own people."

"Perhaps Caesar would be so good as to teach us, from his own extensive experience," Gracchus said with a bland smile to level the acidity of his words.

"I call it love, Gracchus," Commodus said. "I am their father. The people are my children. And I shall hold them to my bosom and embrace them tightly."

"Have you ever embraced someone dying of plague, sire?" Gracchus said.

"No, but if you interrupt me again," Commodus said, "I assure you that *you* shall."

Lucilla intervened before the meeting grew any nastier. "Senators, my brother is very tired," she said, gliding forward smoothly. "Leave your list with me. Caesar will do all that Rome requires." She smiled at them diplomatically, with genuine warmth and respect. "Please escort the senators out," she said to a house slave.

Commodus turned and stalked away to the far side of the room.

The senators bowed. Gracchus met Lucilla's eyes with a smile that underlined his admiration of her political skills and timing. "My lady," he said. "As always, your lightest touch commands obedience."

The senators left, stonefaced. The meeting did not augur well. It was not a good start for a new Emperor. Once they were gone, Commodus turned back to

Lucilla, seething. "Damn them all!" he cursed loudly. "Who are they to lecture me!"

"Commodus," Lucilla said calmly. "The Senate has its uses."

"What uses?" he said. "All they do is talk." He stalked to a window and looked out over the great city, then said with absolute seriousness: "It should be just you, and me, and Rome."

"Don't even think it," Lucilla said. "There's always been a Senate."

"Rome has changed," he answered. "It takes an Emperor to rule an empire."

"Of course. But leave the people their . . ." Lucilla paused, feeling for the right word.

"Illusions?" Commodus said.

"Traditions," Lucilla said with a half smile, giving a more discreet name to Commodus's truth.

It had been a "tradition" for the last two hundred years to give lip service to the notion that the Senate still ruled Rome, through the Emperor. Yet it was a bad joke, they all knew. The army was the true source of Roman political power, and whoever had the Legions in its grasp had Rome by the throat. The trick was never to express the truth aloud to the public, who preferred to fancy themselves a great free republic.

But Commodus was running with a new thought. "My father's war against the barbarians achieved nothing—he said it himself. But the people still loved him."

"The people always love victories," Lucilla said.

"Why?" he said. "They didn't see the battles. What do they care about far-away lands like Germania?"

"They care about the greatness of Rome," Lucilla countered.

"The greatness of Rome! What is that?" Commodus scoffed. "Can I touch it? Where does one find it? Show me the greatness of Rome."

"It's an idea," Lucilla explained. "You can't simply touch it. Greatness is . . . a kind of vision."

"Yes!" Commodus exclaimed. He kissed her on both cheeks in his enthusiasm. "A kind of vision! The very word! Don't you see? I will give the people a newer, greater vision of Rome, and they'll love me for it. They'll soon forget the tedious sermonizing of a few dry old men."

Commodus spread his arms and raised them high. "I will give them the greatest vision of their lives!"

TWENTY-NINE

Street artists were cheerfully at work painting huge gory wall displays: gladiators in mass combat, wild beasts with blood-stained teeth, flashing swords.

Crowds gathered to stare and murmur in pleased anticipation. The advertising campaign for Commodus's new strategy had begun.

Senator Gaius made his way down a street bustling with noonday activity. Small tradesmen and craftsmen peddled their wares, trying to eke a living in these overcrowded, hardscrabble city neighborhoods. An Egyptian clown juggled a dozen eggs. As the senator pushed his way through the throng, a town crier declaimed the latest news, while a hawker pushed a flyer into his hand. Gaius looked at it in irritation: It announced Emperor Commodus's coming games. He hurried on.

He passed a stall where a sudden commotion was flaring up. When he saw that it was two praetorians viciously strong-arming a stallholder, he veered quickly to the far side of the street toward an outdoor café. He glanced back and saw the praetorians dragging the unlucky stallholder away.

"Games!" he complained to Gracchus and the group of senators he joined in the busy café in the heart of the commercial quarter. "One hundred and fifty days of games!"

The senators were sipping their drinks, watching the wall painters at work.

"He's more clever than I thought," Gracchus said quietly.

"Clever?" Gaius said. "The whole of Rome would be laughing at him if they weren't so afraid of his praetorians."

"Fear and wonder," Gracchus said, not without some admiration. "A powerful combination."

"You think people are actually going to be seduced by this, while all Rome goes bankrupt?" Gaius said. "It's madness."

"I think he knows what Rome is," Gracchus replied. "Rome is the mob. He will conjure magic for them and they will be distracted. And he will take their lives. And he will take their freedom. And still they will roar." He shook his head stoically. "The beating heart of Rome isn't the marble of the Senate. It's the sand of the Colosseum. He will give them death. And they will love him for it."

The other senators knew he was right. History had proven it. Bread and circuses won the day. And each new generation of Romans competed with the generation before in demanding ever more grandiose, garish public spectacles. More gladiators killed, more animals slaughtered, more horrific human executions. Ever larger amounts of public money had to go to games and distributions—the free food, cash, and excitement kept the mob mollified.

What the senators didn't know was that Commodus was shooting to surpass anything Rome had seen before. The Emperor Trajan's victory games lasted 120 days, cost four million sesterces, and featured thousands of gladiators and the slaughter of eleven thousand beasts transported from all over the Empire's provinces. Commodus meant to do even better.

And it was all for a coldly practical reason—one it would have brought the senators much discomfort to know.

In Commodus's view, he had no choice but to bypass the feckless, obstructive Senate and go straight to the people for his power. And the games were the key. The people must have their traditions, as Lucilla put it. Who was he to deny his citizens their traditional gladiatorial diversions?

Sitting behind the senators in the marketplace as they ruminated sourly on the macchinations of the new Emperor was a small nondescript man who might have been a sandal maker on midday tea break. His back was to them, but he sat close enough to hear most of what they said. The man kept turning his head in a subtle way so that he could see who among the senators was speaking. The face of this listener was unremarkable save for the deep scar that slanted through the place his right eye used to be. He did not see well with only one eye, but his hearing and memory were sufficiently sharp to make the man a valuable harvester of information. And he was paid well for his gleanings.

THIRTY

People streamed down from their small adobe houses baking on the arid hillsides above the provincial Moroccan town. Nearly all the people who could walk made their way toward the ramshackle arena, hoping for a little drama and some distraction from their austere, difficult lives.

The temperate air and relative quiet of the staging tunnels of the arena belied the stifling heat and the sweat and stink of offal that prevailed just yards away on the arena floor.

Maximus's arm, scarred and gouged where once was emblazoned the proud legionary's tattoo, now had the good fortune of being covered with a bronze arm guard. He had earned this valued bit of protection with his exemplary, ferocious fighting against the *andabatae*—even as he had shed the daub of yellow paint tagging him fodder for sharpened steel. Now he carried a gladiator's red daub.

He strapped the jointed bronze piece of armor into place. Armed and ready, he bent down, picked up some dirt and rubbed it in his hands. He then set off with a fast, deliberate stride through a tunnel split down the middle by iron bars that led to the arena.

Proximo moved with him, walking on the other side of the bars.

Maximus brushed past gladiators who were lined up

along the walls. Some were wounded and were being
attended to by surgeons, while others were just
stunned from a hard-fought previous battle. Others
were still nervously waiting to go on, whispering
prayers.

"All you do is kill, kill, *kill*!" Proximo barked at
him through the bars. "You make it look too easy.
The crowd wants a hero, not a butcher." He threw
his hands up in theatrical frustration. "We want them
to keep coming back. Don't just hack them up so
quickly! Stretch it out!"

The cheers of the crowd grew louder as they neared
the arena.

"Give them an adventure to remember!" Proximo
bellowed above the din. "Fall to one knee—He's
doomed! He doesn't have a prayer!—they'll think.
Then he summons the will—he drags himself up—our
hearts soar—he is victorious!" He was stomping along
his side of the tunnel trying to keep up with Maximus.
"Feel what the crowd wants. Don't just slaughter everyone! Remember—you're an entertainer!"

Without a word to Proximo or a moment's hesitation, Maximus walked out into the glare of the packed
arena. A roar went up the moment he appeared. He
was a known quantity now, a featured combatant. The
Moroccan fans knew they were about to see some
center-ring action.

Out in the blazing sunlight, six opponents awaited.

Maximus sized them up the moment his feet hit the
arena sand. He saw his first target immediately. For
his first assault, he picked out not the smallest opponent nor the one showing the most fear, but the man
who looked the strongest, the most confident, and the
most menacing. When that man went down, Maximus
knew, it would flash in the others' minds that they had
no chance—and they wouldn't.

He waded straight into his opponents, surprising them, separating out a fighter built like a lodgepole pine. He slashed him across the stomach and, when the huge man sank to his knees, Maximus plunged his sword deep into his back. He cut down the rest with the same efficiency, brutally wielding his sword, never giving his opponents a moment's anticipation. One by one they quickly fell. For the last opponent he picked up a second sword from the sand and buried them both into the man's stomach just as he was raising his weapon to strike. Maximus turned away as the man staggered back, blood surging out of his gut. He turned back, yanked out both swords, and with a double swipe, slashed them through the man's neck, beheading him.

The crowd roared its appreciation. Chants of "Spaniard! Spaniard! Spaniard!" rocked the arena. Maximus had cut through his opponents like a scythe through wheat, accomplishing it incredibly fast—the whole clash was over in mere minutes. It was an absolutely stunning feat, and it brought the crowd to its feet.

Proximo, watching the fight from his pavillion, walked out in disgust.

Surrounded by a sea of corpses and gore, Maximus dropped his arms to his side, stepped over a body, and walked toward the tunnel. He threw one of his swords into the pavillion where Proximo had been standing. It clattered among the dignitaries, who took a fearful step back.

The screaming crowd grew silent, watching. Curious.

"Are you not entertained?" he shouted at the crowd. "Are you not entertained? Is this not why you came?" He threw down his other sword and stalked out through the tunnel gates.

THIRTY-ONE

In the cool of the evening, in a rare moment of reflective leisure, Maximus and Juba stood on the high ramparts of Proximo's Gladiator School, looking out at the endless Sahara and the distant mountains. Three dusty riders approaching from afar caught their attention, but they paid them no heed. There always seemed to be people coming to and from the school at all hours—messengers, gamblers, trainers, and fresh slaves.

"My country, it's somewhere out there," Juba said. "My home. My wife is preparing food. My daughters carry water from the river . . . Will I ever see them again? I think no."

"Do you believe you'll meet them again—after you die?" Maximus asked.

"I think so," Juba said. "But then—I will die soon. They will not die for many years."

"But you would wait for them," Maximus said.

"Of course," Juba said. A tentative pause filled the air between the two warriors.

"I would have died in the slave wagon," Maximus said suddenly. "You saved me. I never thanked you." He gave Juba a pained look. "Because my wife, and my son, are waiting for me."

Juba understood and put an affectionate arm around Maximus's broad shoulders. "You'll meet them again," he said. "But not yet, yes?" He gave a hearty laugh: This team was not ready to submit to death just yet.

A clatter of horses' hooves in the courtyard below signaled new arrivals—the three riders they had seen coming from a distance. But as the riders entered the school, they drew attention from all sides, causing a commotion.

The import of the riders' visit to the gladiators became clear later that evening. Two well-armed guards came into the barracks and gestured for Maximus. He got up to follow them. The guards took no chances: They gave this most powerful and brooding of gladiators plenty of space and kept their hands on their weapons as they led him out. Cautiously, they marched him to the director's quarters.

Proximo lounged on a terrace overlooking his compound, sipping wine. A chained hyena sat gnawing a bone in a corner. The two guards entered with their star combatant. Proximo turned and waved the guards away.

"Ah, Spaniard," he said. "Butterfly?" He held out a dish of the honeyed insects.

Maximus shook his head.

"Pity. They're exquisite," the portly impresario said. He popped one into his mouth, savoring its sweet flavor. "So, what do you want? Girl? Boy?"

Maximus just looked at him, almost unemotional, unfeeling. "You sent for me?" he said.

Proximo saw the barely concealed disdain in the man who should be and act like his slave. "You're good, Spaniard," he said. "But you're not that good. That troubles me. You could be magnificent."

"You want me to kill. I kill," Maximus said. "That's enough." He turned to walk out.

"Enough for the provinces," Proximo called after him. "But not for Rome."

Maximus froze in his tracks. Then he turned. "Rome?" he said, suddenly interested.

"My men have just brought the news," Proximo said. "The young Emperor has arranged a series of spectacles in honor of his late father, Marcus Aurelius. I find that amusing, when it was the all-wise Marcus Aurelius who shut us down in the first place. But his day is over now," Proximo said.

"Yes," Maximus said bitterly.

"After five years of scratching around in flea-infested villages," Proximo said with relish, "we're finally going back where we belong. Back to the Colosseum! Ah, Spaniard, wait till you fight in the Colosseum! Fifty thousand Romans following every move of your sword, willing you to deliver that one killing blow. The silence before you strike. The cry that comes after—rising up like a storm! As if you were the thunder god himself." He stopped and looked to the heavens, his eyes shining.

Maximus saw the memories lighting up Proximo's face. "You were once a gladiator," he said.

Proximo turned his eyes to him, coming back to earth. "The best," he said.

"You won your freedom?" Maximus said.

"A long time ago," Proximo replied nostalgically, walking into his chamber and returning with an object. "The Emperor gave me this—the rudius. Just a wooden sword—yet a symbol of your freedom. He touched me on the shoulder and I was free."

Etched into the handle of the sword was Proximo's name and the words "Freeman—By Order of Imperator Marcus Aurelius Antoninus."

"You knew Marcus Aurelius?" Maximus asked, examining the sword, unable to hide the skepticism.

"I didn't say I knew him," Proximo said. "I said he touched me on the shoulder."

Maximo looked at the slave master with calculated scrutiny. "You ask me what I want?" he said. "I, too, want to stand in front of the Emperor, as you did."

"Then listen to me," Proximo said. "Learn from me. I was not the best because I killed quickly, I was the best because the crowd loved me! Win the crowd, and you'll win your freedom."

Maximus heard him now, heard the truth in his words. "I'll win the crowd, then," he said. "I will show them something they've never seen before."

THIRTY-TWO

Traversing the Italian penninsula from the south to the north on the famous Via Appia—the Appian Way—Proximo's slave wagon caravan passed through the small city of Lanuvium south of Rome in early afternoon. It was an undistinguished burg in every other respect save for the fact that it was the birthplace of Rome's most celebrated native son. As the birthplace of Commodus, now Emperor of Rome, Lanuvium inspired Proximo to an act of goodwill and cheer. He broke out an amphora of good Lucanian wine and shared it with his chief subordinates riding on the front platform of the lead slave wagon.

Maximus sat in the back of the same enclosed slave wagon with Juba and several other gladiators. They were allowed no wine. Juba and the others talked about what they knew of Rome—what they had only heard secondhand. None of them had actually been inside the city's great gates.

Maximus himself offered no stories, no opinions.

Juba watched him, knowing there was much knowledge in the man's head he was not revealing.

On the front of the wagon, Proximo raised the wine vessel in a toast to the Emperor as the skyline of the greatest city in the world came into view in the distance. They had finally reached Rome.

THIRTY-THREE

In the chilly air of night, Commodus stood in an upper-floor chamber of the Imperial Palace, lurking like a vampire. He loomed over a bed where an eight-year-old boy slept—Lucius, Lucilla's son. Commodus watched him, ominous and intense. Lucilla soon entered quietly behind him. She stood in the doorway for a moment and watched, disquieted.

Commodus sensed her presence. "He sleeps so well because he is loved," he said without turning to face his sister. He gently reached down and brushed some hair from Lucius's forehead.

Lucilla moved forward quickly.

Feeling the touch, Lucius stirred. "Mother . . . ," Lucius said groggily.

"Go back to sleep," Lucilla cooed, laying a reassuring hand on the boy's shoulder.

"I was dreaming about Father. We were riding horses together . . . ," Lucius said.

"Shh," Lucilla said. "Go back to sleep now." She kissed him on the forehead and straightened his cover.

He soon drifted off once more. She watched him breathe for a moment, already dreaming peacefully again. Turning away she said, "Come, brother . . . it's late," knowing well that Commondus would follow.

Repairing to the grand Imperial bedroom, handsome in its marble columns, classical Greek lines and

plush purple and gold draperies, Commodus sat on his
bed and sighed in irritation. He rummaged through a
pile of scrolls on a bedside table. The scrolls were
covered in plans for the New Rome. More such documents, conveying the gargantuan variety of business
and the economy of the Empire, arrived from the Senate several times a day.

At the marble sideboard, Lucilla prepared a drink
for him, discreetly mixing powder into a medicinal
tonic.

"I will make Rome the wonder of the ages," Commodus boasted. "That's what Gracchus and his cronies
just don't understand." He pushed the scrolls away
from him and rubbed his aching head. "All my own
dreams and desires are splitting my head to pieces."

"Quiet, brother," Lucilla said soothingly as she
stirred his tonic. She then went to him and held out
the drink. "This will help. . . ."

He just looked at her.

She remembered her duties of providing safety for
Commodus in his private chamber, and took a sip of
it herself. Then she handed the concoction to him.
"Yes, just drink this down," she said. She sat comfort-
ingly on the edge of his bed as he drank deeply.

"I think the time is almost right," he said, taking
the cup down from his lips. "I could announce the
dissolution of the Senate at the celebration to honor
our father. Do you think I should? Are the people
ready?"

"We'll talk about it tomorrow," Lucilla said.

"I think they are," he said. "Let those fat jackals
howl from the street corners. Or do you think I should
banish them?"

"I think you should rest now," Lucilla said. She
watched him as he eased back on the bed, his mood
settling. He is a depraved, callow boy, she thought to

herself. Nothing less and nothing more. Rome is in frightening hands. Thank the Gods I am here to control him. Pray to the Gods I can continue to control him.

"Will you stay with me?" Commodus asked.

"Still afraid of the dark, brother?" Lucilla said and smiled gently.

"Still. Always," he said. He shook off the mood and turned to her. "Stay with me tonight," he said with an appealing urgency.

"You know I won't," Lucilla said.

"Then kiss me," Commodus said.

She smiled, kissed his forehead quickly, and then started to go. She stopped at the door and glanced back into the room.

Commodus lay on the bed, a lonely, desperate image.

"Sleep, brother," Lucilla said.

"You know my dreams would terrify the world," Commodus said in a flat voice.

Lucilla left.

THIRTY-FOUR

As the night deepened, Commodus lay for a few moments, unsleeping, his brain feverish with frustrations, plans, and stratagems.

Elsewhere, others found cause to deny sleep for their own reasons. At Senator Gracchus's splendid house on the Palatine Hill, a sedan chair arrived and a cloaked, hooded figure descended from its interior.

A shadowy figure was waiting for her under the portico—Senator Gaius. "Lucilla," he said. He took her arm and led her into the house as if this were a secret romantic assignation.

Though she had not had occasion to visit as an adult, Lucilla knew the interior of Senator Gracchus's house to be a showpiece of Imperial Rome. She found herself walking into an opulent world of beautiful Oriental decadence.

Rich Persian antiques and artwork dotted the candlelit rooms, the first one dominated by a statue of the Persian god of forgiveness, Mithras. Unlike the classical lines of the Imperial Palace, the House of Gracchus favored the luxurious and sybaritic. The household staff, Lucilla noticed, was all male and all young and beautiful.

Gracchus came out to greet Lucilla in the anteroom.

She opened her mouth to speak, then stopped, hesitant to reveal her identity in front of the servants.

"All my servants are deaf and mute," Gracchus said. "How do you think I've stayed alive for so long?"

Lucilla revealed her face from underneath her hood as they began to walk through the house. The servant walked on ahead. Gracchus turned to Lucilla. "Do you know, there was a time, not so very long ago, when I held two children on my knee," he said with a kind smile. "The most beautiful children I'd ever seen. And their father was very proud of them. And I, too, loved them very much, as if they were my own."

"And they loved you," Lucilla said.

"Both of them, for a time . . . ," Gracchus said almost sadly. "I saw one of them grow strong and moral. The other grew . . . dark. I saw his father turn away from him. I saw us all turn away from him. And in his loneliness, I'm sure there were demons."

They moved arm in arm into the central chamber. Senator Gaius followed close behind them. Gracchus poured and handed both his guests glasses of wine.

"They're arresting scholars now!" Lucilla said. "Anyone who dares speak out against the throne— even satirists and chroniclers."

"And mathematicians and Christians," Gaius said in a desolate tone. "All to feed the arena. The Senate did not approve of this martial law. This reign of terror is entirely the praetorians' doing. I'm afraid to go out after dark."

"You should be more afraid of your activities by day," Gracchus said. "The Senate is full of his spies. Led by that whoremaster Falco."

He took a glass of wine for himself. "What is in Commodus's mind?" he asked. "That's what I trouble myself with. He spends his days singularly obsessed— planning the festival to honor your father. He neglects even the most fundamental tasks of government. Just what is it that he's planning?"

"And what pays for it all?" Gracchus queried. "These daily games are costing a fortune and yet we have instituted no new taxes."

"The future," Lucilla answered. "The future pays for it all . . ." She looked at them ruefully. "He's started selling the grain reserves."

"This can't be true," Gaius said, stunned.

"The people will be starving in two years," Lucilla said. "I hope they're enjoying the spectacles, because soon enough they'll be dead because of them."

"Rome must know this," Gaius said, throwing his hands up in dismay.

"And how?" Lucilla said. "He's going to dissolve the Senate. Then who will tell them before it's too late? You, Gracchus? Or you, Gaius? Will you make a speech on the floor of the Senate denouncing my brother? And then see your family in the Colosseum to face the lions? Who would dare?"

She looked back and forth at the two men, gauging their resolve. "He must die," she said simply.

Her words sank in.

"Quintus and his praetorians would simply seize control themselves," Gaius said.

"No," Lucilla said. "Cut off the head and the snake cannot strike."

"Lucilla, Gaius is right," Gracchus interjected. "Until we can neutralize the praetorians, we can achieve nothing."

"Besides, we haven't enough men," Gaius said.

"So we do nothing?" Lucilla said.

"No, child, we keep our counsel and we prepare," Gracchus said. "As long as the people support him, we are voices without steel. We are but air. But every day that passes, he makes more enemies. One day he will have more enemies than friends—and then we will act. Then we will strike. Until then . . . we must be docile. We are obedient, yet we are treacherous."

In the Imperial Palace, Marcus Aurelius Commodus Antoninus, Emperor of Rome, was now sleeping.

THIRTY-FIVE

Though they were on its very outskirts by late afternoon, Maximus, Juba, and the other gladiators saw almost nothing of the Eternal City from within the covered slave wagon.

Proximo, reclining at the front of the wagon, saw it all too clearly. Something had changed since he left five years before. Rome was now an armed camp.

A large, intimidating praetorian unit guarded an impressive gate into the city, now like a military checkpoint.

The wagon stopped at the gate. A praetorian captain moved to Proximo. "Papers," the praetorian captain demanded.

Proximo gave him some small documents. The praetorian studied them as other praetorians pulled up the woven tarps covering the back of the wagon and peered in at the gladiators.

A praetorian looked at Maximus deeply. Maximus returned his stare. Did he detect a flicker of recognition from the praetorian? But the guard moved on to look at the next gladiator.

A family of refugees were out of their wagon, kneeling in the road in front of the praetorians. An officer was explaining that the refugees were going to have to produce some kind of tribute before being allowed into the city.

The captain waved Proximo's wagons through. The praetorians at the back of Maximus's wagon lowered the tarps again. The wagon continued on through the ranks of stern *praetoriani* and into the city.

Proximo grew more apprehensive as his wagon train rolled through a Rome that appeared far poorer and dirtier than he ever remembered it. Cleanliness was a tradition of the Roman people. What did this run-down condition of the neighborhoods say about city services under the new Emperor, and about the morale of his citizens?

Worse still, what could he expect to find at the compound he had been forced to lock up and leave five years before?

With bated breath he rode the slave wagons up to the gates of the grand Roman compound housing Proximo's old school. He saw with relief that the buildings were still standing, and that the imposing gates were still locked tight.

He threw down the keys to one of his guards, who unlocked the heavy barred gates and pushed them open. As Proximo's wagons drove in, the trainer looked around giddily: He was home. Back in his own little kingdom. And his kingdom still looked to be in one piece.

Maximus and the other gladiators were just glad to be let out of their box. They looked around curiously as they were led out of the slave wagons into a large open courtyard inside the now-locked gates. It looked to them like Proximo's Moroccan school, yet it was much more impressive. A marble fountain with an enormous statue of the war god Mars towered at the center of the compound.

But as the gladiators climbed down from the wagon, stretching after the long arduous journey, it was not the statue or the rather grand school compound that drew their attention. Across the rooftops of Rome, not two or three blocks in the distance, there rose up an awesome structure that blotted out part of the sky: the venerated Colosseum.

From it came a low constant roar: the sound of fifty-six thousand voices baying for blood.

Maximus, Juba, and the others stared at the monumental edifice, lighted up like Jupiter's very palace, and listened to the rising and falling voice of the crowd. Each man was thinking, Is that where I die?

"Have you ever seen anything like that before?" Juba asked. "I didn't know men could build such things."

Proximo, following his past usual custom, waded through the fountain to lean over and kiss the toe of Mars, his own protector god. Looking up at the powerful carved figure, he murmured, "Good to see you again, old friend. Bring me fortune."

As he rose again, a great shout went up from the looming Colosseum, and the cries formed into a chant: "Hail Caesar! Hail Caesar!" To Proximo and his lieutenants familiar with Colosseum games, it was evident what was happening: The Emperor had just arrived.

Proximo waded back out of the fountain, his eyes shining, murmuring the cry along with the distant crowd. "Hail Caesar! Hail Caesar!" He stared at the hypnotic sight of the immense Colosseum, where the crowds continued to chant, "Hail Caesar! Hail Caesar!"

His eyes reached for Maximus, as if to say, There he is, the man who can set you free. "Win the crowd," Proximo reminded him.

Maximus met his look, and Proximo read his reaction as being seduced by the majesty of the colossal arena glowing in the night, the ex-general buying into the promise of freedom for the right performer. Proximo read Maximus wrong.

Maximus had only one thought as he gazed at the Colosseum: *He is there. He is close. The moment is approaching, and soon I will see him for myself: the man I live to kill.*

THIRTY-SIX

With the burning, late-morning sun bleaching out the shadows and creating a shimmer of glare over the towering parapets, Maximus and the other gladiators had to shade their eyes to see the top of the Colosseum as their slave cart approached the foot of the building. High above the empty arena, they could see slaves balancing on high beams, crawling out on ropes, and unrolling huge rolls of silk—sun tarps that would provide shade for the wealthier patrons' seats below.

In the quarter all around the spectacular site, the energy mounted as the hour of the games drew near. The provincial gladiators watched everything in awe. Commerce and hucksterism in all their forms thrived.

Merchants opened up their stalls in the curved arcade around the outside of the Colosseum, offering for sale everything from food to magic elixirs, from toys to aphrodisiacs. A constant din rose up as they extolled and demonstrated the virtues of their products.

Gangs of whores of both sexes crawled the streets. They had bizarrely colored hair and elaborate makeup, and they plied the oldest profession with unusual gaiety and panache in the festival atmosphere.

Citizens began arriving, pushing past the vendors and the pickpockets—whole families with picnic lunches and pillows on which to get comfortable, carrying swollen wine skins.

Trainers delivered ferocious animals into the Colosseum in barred cages—African lions, hyenas, spotted leopards, Caledonian bears, sharp-tusked wild boars. These beasts were destined either for ritual slaughter in the morning show, or meant to perform the public execution of low-status criminals during the lunch break, all before the gladiatorial main event of the afternoon.

In the busy arcade, barbers and bloodletters practiced their craft alongside exotic alchemists, fire eaters, and contortionists.

Gamblers crowded betting booths and haggled mercilessly.

Richer citizens arrived in sedan chairs and litters, feigning indifference to the hooting, excited mob.

Mounted Praetorian Guard units cantered in sizeable numbers throughout the quarter, trying to retain some semblance of order.

Maximus and the other gladiators were ushered by Proximo's guards down a long interior ramp and past countless animal cages into the bowels of the amphitheater. The interior of the Colosseum was a warren of halls and cells and passageways and staging areas—as busy a world as the one bustling outside.

And where the warriors went—their dressing and armoring areas, trainers' rooms and ready stations—gamblers went too, circulating everywhere, observing the fighters, picking up inside information, angling for the best odds on the best matches.

Maximus and the other combatants were led ever deeper into the cool innards of the Colosseum, to a whole new subterranean realm. Numerous holding cells lined the walls. Racks and racks of shiny weaponry and polished armor filled prep rooms.

And, most striking of all, everywhere around them was the heavy machinery of the spectacles above. Huge, creaking "elevator" platforms and ramps and pulleys and counterweights were being manned by teams of constantly working, sweating slaves.

Finally, Proximo's guards led the gladiators into the arcade cells, a series of cages with barred fronts open to the public. As is the paddock at a race course, the new fighters were on view to a gawking crowd of fight fans and gamblers.

As Maximus made his way through the open-fronted cells, his attention swung to the loud voices of Proximo and Cassius, the Colosseum's head impresario.

"The Emperor wants *battles*?!" Proximo said incredulously. "I refuse to squander my best fighters." His men were highly trained single-combat warriors, not meant to be wasted in staged mass battle scenes.

"The crowd wants battles, so the Emperor gives them battles," Cassius replied, "and you are assigned to replicate the battle of Carthage."

"You mean the massacre of Carthage!" Proximo said.

Maximus was ordered to stop in one of the cells. He settled down as far from the staring, hooting crowd as he could, not wanting to attract attention.

Proximo and Cassius moved away, with Proximo still complaining loudly. "Why don't you go to the prisons?" he said. "Round up some thieves and beggars for this mindless slaughter."

"We've already done that," Cassius said.

"If you want to just waste the best gladiators in the Empire," Proximo said, "I want double rates."

But he was spitting against the wind.

"You'll get the contract rates or you'll get your contract canceled," Cassius replied, losing his patience.

"You don't like it, crawl back down the shit-hole you came from."

Among the crowd drifting past the gladiator cages were some boys from noble families, watched over by their servants. One of the boys walked up to the bars, gaped for a while at the massive form of Haken, and then walked on.

Maximus paid no attention to the passing crowd; he was listening to the fading voices of Proximo and Cassius. A far closer voice suddenly made him turn his head.

"Gladiator!" Lucius called out.

It was one of the boys, a fair-haired lad with a pleasant manner. Maximus had no idea who he was, but his eye was drawn to him. With the confidence of a young aristocrat, the boy beckoned the fighting man to come closer to the bars.

"Gladiator, are you the one they call the Spaniard?" Lucius asked.

Something about the direct, mannerly comportment of the boy stirred Maximus's memory of his own son. He moved closer to the youth. "Yes," he said.

"They said you were a giant," Lucius said. "They said you could crush a man's skull with just one hand."

Maximus spread his hand, and looked down at it. "A man's? No . . . ," he said. He held his hand out to Lucius, with a grin. "But a boy's . . ."

Lucius liked that: He smiled back, humored. He pointed to the raised horse figures on Maximus's bronze breastplate. "Do they have good horses in Spain?" Lucius said.

Maximus smiled at his youthful show of expertise. "Some of the best," he said, indicating the figures. "This was Argento. This was Scato. They were my horses. They were taken from me."

"I like you, Spaniard," Lucius said. "I shall cheer for you."

"They let you watch the games?" Maximus asked the boy.

"My uncle says it makes me strong," Lucius replied.

"But what does your father say?" Maximus said.

"My father's dead," Lucius said.

Lucius's servant came up to the boy and bowed with humble respect. "Master Lucius. It's time," the servant said.

"I have to go," Lucius said to Maximus.

"Your name's Lucius?" Maximus said.

"Lucius Verus, after my father," Lucius said proudly. The boy turned and left, followed by his servant.

A lightning strike of recognition suddenly ripped through Maximus. He stared after the boy, stunned, realizing he must be Lucilla's boy. He searched the crowd—was Lucilla somewhere out there? He saw only the gaping faces of the fight fans, now whipped into an expectant frenzy for the upcoming battle.

THIRTY-SEVEN

The holding cells were at surface level, right at the edge of the arena, the final arming area before the warriors left to go out on to the big stage. Racks of helmets, body armor, and weapons waited to be issued. Beyond, through bars, onlookers could watch as a cage of eight lions was prepared—cruelly baited and goaded—before they were released into the arena.

Proximo's guards led the gladiators into this final space. Barred windows offered a ground-level view of the action in the broad, sandy arena.

Maximus entered with the rest of the combatants. He walked over to a window and looked out at the sweep of sand that seemed to stretch out forever. He could see a narrow section of the stands, hear the sounds of the stadium filling up. A group of Christians were kneeling together in prayer at one end of the expanse.

Maximus stepped away from the window as the gates were raised and the lions were released up the ramps.

Very quickly, screams pierced the air and the crowd began to give voice to their horror and pleasure.

As the guards prepared the gladiators, handing out armor, Maximus spoke in a low hush to one of the giant officials of the arena. "Is the Emperor here?" Maximus asked him.

"He'll be here," the giant official said. "He comes every day."

Maximus turned and found one of the guards holding out a helmet to him. Ignoring the offer, he moved over to the rack of helmets and ran his eye over them. He picked out one that had a fuller face guard, and tried it on.

As he turned his head back toward the arena, he looked fierce, determined . . . and anonymous.

Proximo's well-schooled, highly regarded gladiators—Maximus, Juba, and Haken among them—were now armored and costumed. They were dressed to look like Carthaginian desert warriors. All wore mask-like helmets in the shape of freakish animal heads, and carried long North African tribal spears with barbed points at both ends, as well as long, curved, heavy shields.

They were lined up in a ramp leading up to the arena, Proximo standing with them.

"You have the honor of fighting in front of the Emperor himself," the official reminded them. "When the Emperor enters, you raise your weapons in salute."

Trumpets began sounding from the grand arch.

"When you salute him, speak together," he said. "Face the Emperor. Don't turn your backs."

More trumpets blared from above. Drums began to roll like thunder.

"Go," Proximo said. "Die with honor."

Proximo eyed each gladiator as he passed—taking a long steady look at Maximus. His five best gladiators walked up the ramp to meet their fate.

Maximus stepped out at last onto the floor of the mighty Colosseum arena. Nothing he could possibly imagine could have prepared him for the sight of the thousands upon thousands of screaming spectators, row after row of cheering faces mounting up tier after tier, everywhere he turned, like a surging tide. He was staggered.

The gladiators took up somewhat of a loose formation in the center sand.

Simultaneously, three other teams appeared from different entrances into the arena. A total of twenty gladiators were now on the Colosseum stage. They all wore striking Carthaginian armor and carried long double-pointed spears and heavy metal shields.

The combatants lined up and faced the Imperial box, which so far remained empty. Elevated fifteen feet above the arena floor, it sat dramatically at the top of a sheer black marble wall. There was no mistaking that it was the Emperor's seat.

A cohort of fifty menacing Praetorian Guard archers surrounded the box.

Commodus's personal bodyguard of six centurions stood at the edges of the box itself, eyes constantly watching for assassins or any other threat like trained guarddogs.

Then Commodus and Lucilla entered—and the crowd went wild, rising as one and yelling salutes.

Lucilla, accompanied by Lucius, went to her seat.

Commodus moved to the edge of the Imperial box and savored the adulation of his people. He raised his arms and played at being the humble and benevolent monarch. The crowd cheered him, awashing him with praise.

Gaius and other senators in the stands nearby saw this and tried not to show how ill at ease it made them feel. The latest outrageous news had just passed among them: Commodus had begun seizing the property of out-of-favor senators to replenish the dwindling treasury that was paying for these lavish games. The youthful Emperor was even planning to ask the Senate to rename Rome "Commodiana," and designate it his own personal colony. He now egotistically required his praetorian training partners to address him as Hercules, son of Jupiter.

Commodus looked down at the gladiators—he seemed to stare straight at Maximus, as if to see right through the grill of his mask.

Maximus was frozen for a moment, overwhelmed with hatred as he stared up at the man he longed to put to death. To one side of Commodus, he saw Quintus. On the other side stood Lucilla and Lucius. Maximus took in the impossible distance, the praetorian archers, the centurion bodyguards.

On a signal from Cassius, the gladiators below all saluted with their weapons and shouted, "*Ave, Caesar—Morituri te Salutamus!*"—"*We who are about to die salute you!*" Only Maximus remained silent.

The crowd roared at the tops of their voices. Commodus beamed, and sat regally. Lucilla was positioned beside him, with Lucius on her other side.

Then Cassius, the Colosseum master of ceremonies, stepped forward and orated to the crowd in his powerful voice: "On this day we reach back to hallowed antiquity to bring you a re-creation of—*the second fall of mighty Carthage!*"

A fanfare sounded from the trumpets, accompanied by a rolling, pulsing drumbeat. The crowd cheered loudly. This is what they had come for: A true spectacle! A drama, a great gaudy production full of blood, ringing steel, and shocking novelty.

"On the barren plain of Zama," Cassius went on, "stood the invincible armies of the barbarian Hannibal! Ferocious mercenaries and warriors of all brute nations bent on merciless conquest! Your Emperor is pleased to give you . . . *the barbarian horde!*"

He gestured to the gladiators in the arena. The crowd laughed and jeered at the costumed "barbarians."

The drummers began pounding out a more insistent, heroic beat.

"But on that illustrious day," Cassius declaimed, "the Gods sent against them Rome's greatest warriors who would on this day, and on these same arid Numidian deserts, decide *the fate of the empire*! Your Emperor is pleased to give you . . . *the legionaries of Scipio Africanus*!"

THIRTY-EIGHT

The crowd exploded as the huge doors at the ends of the arena suddenly burst open and six chariots thundered in from each end. Each chariot had a driver and an archer or a lance man. All were dressed in grand, theatrical versions of the familiar Roman legionary's *lorica segmentata.*

The chariots stormed through the line of gladiators as the warriors scattered to avoid them. They then turned and made a second pass, running over one gladiator in the process. The vehicles then raced in the opposite direction around the outside of the arena, herding the twenty gladiators toward the center. A cloud of dust and sand obscured the gladiators' vision as the trumpets and drums whipped the crowd to an elevated frenzy.

Maximus assessed the situation and their vulnerability. As the juggernauts spun past, he turned around almost by instinct, and saw a spear flying through the dust.

The spear sliced through a gladiator's neck, killing him instantly. He fell, ungainly and hard, blood bubbling through his wound.

Maximus instantly took control, calling to the other gladiators: "If we work together, we can win!" He motioned them into a staggered column formation.

"Close ranks! Shields together! Lock the formation! Shoulders in to the shields!" The gladiators responded to his authoritative voice and formed up—all except Haken, who stood outside the formation, ready to fight his own individual battle, wanting to claim his own heroism.

The crowd was amazed, seeing the warriors work together—they had never seen gladiators do anything like this! Neither had the charioteers. They spun around the outside of the formation, occasionally firing arrows and spears that sliced harmlessly into the gladiators' shields.

Little Lucius was standing and cheering his head off for his new hero and friend down in the arena.

Haken had his own fans, who cheered his every move as he braced for a chariot attack.

Two chariots peeled off from the outside and galloped toward the center of the arena, probing the defenses of the formation. The sharpened wheel blades of the chariots snapped off gladiators' spears as they roared by.

At Maximus's command, the gladiators formed themselves into a diamond formation.

Two more chariots peeled off as the other two returned to the outside of the racetrack. The chariots galloped straight toward the gladiators. One chariot veered off to the left. The other aimed for the right-hand corner of the diamond, the driver counting on his wheel blades to make mincemeat of the men in that part of the formation.

As the chariot neared, at Maximus's word, the gladiators suddenly changed their formation into the *testudo*, the tortoise, which looked like a tight shell with shields covering the top as well as the sides. The chariot smashed into the corner of the *testudo*, one wheel riding harmlessly up over the shields, throwing the speeding vehicle onto its side in a violent sliding crash, spitting the driver and archer out into the sand.

Haken ran up to collect the fallen weapons and was hit in the leg by an arrow. He buckled, and fell. The second chariot wheeled and bore down on him. Juba hurled his spear, slicing the chariot's driver in the back, knocking him out of the chariot.

Maximus left the formation to rescue Haken, pulling him flat to the ground as another hurtling chariot flashed by, its wheel blades just passing over Haken's head.

The same wheel blades sliced into the driver of the crashed chariot, who was trying to crawl away, severing his torso in half.

The runaway second chariot ran into a third chariot on the outside track, sending them both crashing into the gate, killing the third driver and his spearman in the crush.

Maximus ran for one of the broken chariots and cut the horse free. The other gladiators covered him as he leapt on the horse's back and spurred off. Once mounted on the big white stallion, he was again the ruthless dealer of death of the Felix Regiment. He veered and galloped hard in pursuit of the remaining chariots, singling one out.

As the driver realized he was suddenly the prey, he whipped his horses up and raced hard, keeping his fearful eyes locked on Maximus. He failed to see the archer from the first wrecked chariot, who was running along the wall trying to escape. He crushed the man between the wheels of his chariot and the arena wall just as Maximus galloped past and swung his sword, killing him in an instant with his sharp blade. The chariot smashed into the wall with phenomenal velocity, its splintered parts careening into the crowd.

The gladiators dragged two wrecked chariots onto the path of the racetrack to slow the other circling vehicles.

Maximus, chasing another chariot, leaned down from the horse and plucked up a thrown spear sticking out of the sand. He gained on the chariot and flung the spear with such incredible force it went through both the spearman and the driver, piercing both armor and vital organs.

Another chariot swung in behind Maximus and was hard on his heels. The driver was about to slash at him, when Maximus galloped straight at one of the wrecks and jumped his horse over it. The pursuer didn't see the wreck in time and smashed into it, the chariot somersaulting end over end.

Maximus wheeled his horse at the end of the stadium and started back toward two chariots bearing down on him in staggered formation. They sped toward each other much like Medieval jousters. They flashed together for an instant. Maximus deftly jumped the wheel blade of one chariot while decapitating the driver of the other. He turned and threw his sword into the first driver, whose chariot slammed into a pillar, killing both himself and his archer.

Gladiators swarmed in on the remaining chariot teams, executing them with brutal singlemindedness.

Maximus pulled up his horse and glanced around. All of his opponents were defeated. He dismounted as his group of gladiators moved in on either side of him, bloody and sweaty, proud and victorious.

Haken was among them.

In the stands, the mob was overjoyed. A praetorian exchanged a quick glance with a comrade, impressed by Maximus's feats.

In the arena, Maximus, for the first time as a combatant, raised his right arm, holding his sword high in the traditional gladiator's sign of triumph over death. The crowd wildly applauded his brave, electrifying victory.

THIRTY-NINE

In the Imperial box, Lucius was wild with admiration. Lucilla was staring at the helmeted hero.

Commodus gestured to the Colosseum master of ceremonies, Cassius, to join him. The Emperor appeared to be in very good form. "My history is a little hazy, Cassius," he said jovially, "but shouldn't the barbarians *lose* the battle of Carthage?"

"Yes, sire. Forgive me, sire," Cassius said deferentially, terrified, his voice shaking. Men had been executed *ad bestia*—thrown to the lions—for less.

"Oh, I'm not disappointed," Commodus said. "I rather enjoy surprises." He pointed to Maximus. "Who is he?"

"They call him the Spaniard, sire," Cassius said, able to breathe once again.

"I think I'll meet him," Commodus said.

"Yes, sire," Cassius replied, and went off to fetch Maximus.

Maximus and the other gladiators took in the cheers of the crowd as they moved toward the gate.

Suddenly two groups of black-garbed praetorians ran in from either end of the arena and surrounded the fighters. A captain emerged from a small side gate and called out to the men, "Drop your weapons!"

The gladiators dropped their swords and spears.

"You, gladiator," the captain said to Maximus. "The Emperor has asked for you."

"I am at the Emperor's service," Maximus replied, his heart leaping in his chest. This was the moment he had waited for. He turned to see Commodus walking out onto the sand, smiling at him. This would be his chance.

Seeing a broken arrow half buried in the sand, Maximus quickly knelt. As the other gladiators knelt too, Maximus slowly closed his fist around the broken arrow shaft.

Commodus came closer and closer still, smiling, his entourage surrounding him. Maximus saw Lucilla watching from the box above. He heard himself breathing heavily in his helmet mask. He gathered himself . . . nearly there . . . Commodus with a smile of greeting . . . closer now . . . almost within striking distance. He readied his arm for the blow . . .

Suddenly Lucius, running from the stands, dashed around the entourage and grabbed Commodus by the hand.

Commodus laughed and moved the boy in front of him, facing the gladiator hero. "Rise, rise," he beckoned to Maximus. "Your fame is well deserved, Spaniard. I don't think there's ever been a gladiator to match you. . . . And as for this young man! He insists you are Hector reborn—or is it Hercules?"

Maximus could not strike. Lucius was in the way.

"But why doesn't the hero reveal himself and tell us all his real name?" Commodus said.

Maximus stood very still, saying nothing. The sound of his breathing intensified.

"You do have a name?" Commodus urged.

"My name is Gladiator," Maximus said. Then he turned and walked away.

Turning one's back on the Emperor was an unimaginable insult. The crowd gasped audibly.

"How dare you show your back to me!" Commodus spat.

But Maximus kept walking across the sand.

Commodus nodded to Quintus, Commander of the Guard, who gestured an order to his praetorians.

The crowd watched, tense and silent.

A squad of praetorians marched into the arena, blocking Maximus's exit. They stood facing him, swords out.

Finally, Maximus stopped.

Commodus spoke calmly and clearly. "Slave," he seethed. "You will remove your helmet and tell me your name."

Slowly, Maximus turned back to face him. He knew he had no choice now. Slowly, he raised his hands to his helmet mask. Then in one rapid move, the mask was off.

Commodus stared, stunned.

Quintus gaped.

Lucilla put her hand over her mouth in amazement.

Maximus spoke out in a clear, proud voice: "My name is Maximus Decimus Meridas, Commander of the Army of the North, General of the Western Armies, loyal servant to the true Emperor, Marcus Aurelius," Maximus said.

Stunned silence swept the Colosseum.

Then he turned to Commodus directly, and speaking more quietly but in deadly earnest to the man he knew would soon have him killed, he made his last act of defiant will: "I am father to a murdered son, husband to a murdered wife, and I will have vengeance in this life, or the next."

Maximus and Commodus locked eyes in mutual hatred.

Then Commodus gave a sign to his praetorians.

"Arms!" Quintus said. The praetorians drew their swords and closed in on Maximus.

The crowd reacted with a storm of booing, yelling their disapproval. They reached out a forest of raised thumbs, meaning, Let him live!

The praetorians hesitated, blades drawn, unsure what to do, looking to the Emperor for his command.

Commodus looked around at the people of Rome, astonished, concealing his fury. His own crowd—cheering for his mortal enemy?

Slowly, with supreme difficulty, he forced his features into a smile. Acting the gracious and merciful Emperor, he raised his thumb.

And the crowd let out a great roar of approval. A chant went up: *"Maximus! Maximus! Maximus! . . ."*

Lucilla saw it, amazed. Gaius and the senators stepped back, taking in the crowd's enthusiastic cheers.

Never in the long, long history of the Colosseum had they ever seen such a thing!

Watching from the stands was another face that was blank with astonishment. It was Cicero, Maximus's manservant in the army. He watched his former master with disbelief, his mind tumbling over itself with possibilities.

Maximus turned and led his gladiators to the ramp leading out of the arena, striding away in the midst of swirling chaos. Arena guards and praetorians tried to keep order, but the crowd poured in from the arena end as other gladiators mobbed upward from inside.

Maximus pushed through the throng and was about to leave the ramp. But he paused and turned back, drawn by the sheer volume of the cheers echoing around the great amphitheater. As he looked back with a granite look in his eyes, he thought: *The battle isn't over yet.*

FORTY

The Emperor of Rome walked into the palace statue room still dressed from the arena in his grand purple and gold vestments, the dust of the Colosseum sand on the soles of his sandals. Trembling, barely under control, he crossed the ancient chamber that housed two giant statues of the gods Hercules and Verinium.

He approached the bust of Marcus Aurelius and stared at it harshly. He let out a shriek and exploded in rage. He hacked at the black marble head of his father with his *gladius*, sparks shooting up from the blade. Commodus howled out his outrage like a child.

Then all grew deadly silent.

FORTY-ONE

.

It was business as usual at dinnertime at Proximo's Gladiator School. The men collected their food one-by-one from a hatchway.

Haken and Juba sat down along the same bench with Maximus. Haken and Juba began tucking into their food heartily.

"Maximus?" Haken said between huge mouthfuls.

"Yes," Maximus replied. He did not yet have any food.

"You commanded Legions?" the big German asked. "You had many victories?"

"Yes," Maximus said.

"In Germania?" Haken said pointedly.

"In many countries," Maximus responded.

Haken looked at him steadily.

"General!" the cook called from behind the hatchway.

Maximus got up and took his bowl of food and sat back down to eat. He hesitated, staring down at the food, wondering of its contents.

Juba saw his hesitation. "You have a great name now," he said reassuringly. "He must kill your name before he can kill you."

Still Maximus balked, staring into the bowl.

Haken, watching this, reached over and took a heaping spoonful of Maximus's food and ate it. He gave Maximus a look: So there—Then he began to violently cough and started to choke, bending over holding his throat in the throes of poison.

Suddenly, he stopped convulsing, and then started to laugh in good cheer. Maximus and the others joined in chuckling at the huge German's joke.

FORTY-TWO

Lucilla moved quickly down a long corridor in the dark palace. Tense, she stopped before the doors to the throne room. She braced herself before she entered.

Commodus sat calmly at his desk, signing papers. Absorbed, he moved from one sheet to the other, signing, while a scribe looked on.

Lucilla was surprised to find him not raging, as he had been the last few days. She walked up to the desk.

He turned and looked at her. "Why is he still alive?" he demanded.

"I don't know," she said.

"He shouldn't be alive," her brother said. "That vexes me. I am terribly vexed."

Lucilla watched him cautiously, expecting an explosion.

Commodus dismissed the scribe. He got up and walked past her. "I did what I had to do," he said, turning back toward her. "If Father had had his way, the Empire would have been torn apart. You do understand that, don't you?"

"Yes," Lucilla replied.

"What did you feel, when you saw him?" Commodus said, watching her face closely.

"I felt nothing," Lucilla said carefully.

"He wounded you deeply, didn't he?"

"Not more than I wounded him."

She said it so coldly that Commodus seemed convinced. He moved over to the tall window and looked out at nighttime Rome. "They lied to me in Germania," he said. "They told me he was dead. If they lie to me, they don't respect me. If they don't respect me, how can they ever love me?"

"You have to let the Legions know that treachery will not go unpunished," Lucilla said.

Commodus gazed at her in admiration. "Dear sister, I wouldn't want to be your enemy."

"Then what are you going to do?" Lucilla asked.

FORTY-THREE

Maximus was lying awake on the bed in his darkened cell when he heard a guard approaching. He leapt to his feet at once, expecting assassins.

The guard entered his cell and unlocked his chain. "This way," the guard ordered. He took Maximus out into the corridor. Maximus walked before him, alert to every move, tensed for the sudden strike in the back, the mass overpowering assault.

The guard led Maximus into an empty cell farther down the corridor and shackled him to the wall once more. Then the guard turned and left.

And into the light stepped a cloaked and hooded woman. Lucilla.

Maximus stared at her, his face hardening.

"Rich matrons pay well to be pleasured by the bravest of champions," Lucilla said coyly.

Maximus fought the urge to strangle her on the spot. "I knew your brother would send assassins," he said. "I didn't think he would send his best."

"Maximus, he doesn't know—" Lucilla began.

"My family was burnt and my son was crucified while he was still alive!" Maximus interrupted, spitting out his words like venom.

"I knew nothing of that," she said. "You must believe me."

"Don't lie to me," he said.

"I have wept for them," she said.

"As you wept for your father?" Maximus sneered. He lunged at her, his hands pinned behind him, held back only by the chain bolted to the wall.

"I have been living in a prison of fear since that day," Lucilla said, anguished. "To be unable to mourn your father for fear of your brother's retribution. To live in terror every minute of every day because your son is heir to the throne . . . I have wept for them all."

"My son was innocent," Maximus said.

"So is mine," Lucilla said vehemently.

Maximus stared at her, breathing hard. And at long last, he slowly relaxed.

"Must my son die, too, before you'll trust me?" she said.

Maximus turned his face away, filled with black bitterness. "Why does it matter if I trust you or not?" he said.

"The Gods have spared you," she said. "Don't you understand? Today I saw a slave become more powerful than the Emperor of Rome."

"The Gods have spared me what?" he said. "I am at their mercy. With the power only to amuse a mob."

"*That* is power!" she said. "The mob *is* Rome. While Commodus controls them, he controls everything." She lowered her tone, trying desperately to reach him. "Listen to me. My brother has many enemies, most of all in the Senate. But while the people followed him, no one dared stand up to him—until you."

"They oppose Commodus, but they do nothing," Maximus said.

"There are some politicians who have dedicated their lives to Rome," Lucilla said. "One man above all. If I can arrange it, will you meet him?"

Maximus stared at her. "Do you not understand?"

he said. "I may be killed in this cell tonight. Or in the arena tomorrow. I'm just a slave now. What possible difference can I make?"

"This man wants what you want," Lucilla said.

"Then let *him* kill Commodus!" Maximus said in rage.

As she looked at him, she saw he was closed against anything she could say, any idea she could possibly present. "I knew a man once," she said, "a noble man . . . a man of principle who loved my father and my father loved him, and this man served Rome well!"

"That man is gone," Maximus said harshly. "Your brother did his work well."

"Let me help you," Lucilla said, making him face her.

"Yes, you can help me," he said. "Forget you ever knew me. Never come here again."

He rattled on the barred door. "Guard!" he said. "The lady has finished with me."

The guard unlocked the door and led Maximus out of the cell.

FORTY-FOUR

A young legionary officer stood stiffly to attention in the hot sun of the Imperial courtyard. Not a breeze stirred in the closed-in quadrangle.

"What's your name?" Commodus said.

"Julian Crassus, sire," the officer said, frightened in the presence of the august ruler.

"How long were you in Germania?" Commodus said.

"Two years," young Crassus said. He was dripping sweat.

A second legionary officer stood rigidly next to the first. Commodus moved over to face him. "And your name?" he asked.

"Marcus, sire," the second officer said, his voice nervously wavering.

"My father's name," Commodus said, with amused irony.

"I served him with pride for twenty-three years, sire," Marcus said, his voice stronger now.

Commodus nodded and joined a very jittery Quintus, who watched from the side in the shade of a tall statue of the Emperor Trajan. Beyond Quintus stood a firing squad of praetorian archers, their powerful longbows at their sides.

"They must have known of Maximus's escape,"

Commodus said to Quintus. "When did they find the bodies of the four others?"

"They thought it was a barbarian raid," Quintus said, tight-lipped. "Four of our best men were killed."

Commodus just stared darkly at him.

"These are good men," Quintus said, meaning the two anxious, grim-faced legionary officers standing at attention behind them. "Loyal to the Emperor."

Commodus went on glaring at him, and considered the argument. Then he gave a sudden nod to the captain of the archers.

"Load your arrows, prepare to fire," the captain said.

The archers at once nocked arrows and drew their bows.

Commodus had a new thought. He put his arm around Quintus and walked the commander of the Praetorian Guards in front of the drawn bows. "Then perhaps it was you who knew and never told me," he said. "Which is it, Quintus?"

"I . . . didn't know," Quintus stammered.

"You didn't know?" Commodus said sarcastically. "But a general is always in control. Always in command."

"Yes, Caesar," Quintus said.

Commodus stared at Quintus. Then he placed himself between the two legionaries facing the archers, who were now trembling under the strain of their drawn bows. He put his arms around the young officers, and kissed first one on the cheek, then the other.

"Then give the command," Commodus said.

Shaking, Quintus walked out of the line of fire, turned, and looked at the Emperor standing between the two victims. He could not do it.

"Say it—*General*," Commodus mocked.

Quintus drew himself erect, and barked, "Fire!"

The archers fired. The two legionaries, shot all the way through their chests with war arrows, sagged and fell. Commodus stepped out from between them and strode away, untouched.

FORTY-FIVE

A cloaked Senator Gracchus slowly climbed a long stairway inside the Colosseum, dust falling from the tiers above. As he listened to the roaring crowd inside, neither his gait nor his face reflected enthusiasm for this outing.

He emerged out on one of the shaded top tiers and looked down into the arena. The Colosseum was packed with cheering, yelling, celebrating Romans. They did not seem an oppressed or a dreary or an undernourished throng, rather a people delighted to have the chance to escape into the kind of gory entertainment they craved.

It was the end of one event, and teams of slaves were cleaning up the arena after a particularly bloody bout. One squad hooked human carcasses to mules and hauled them off, picking up severed limbs as they went. Another team tossed down fresh sand to cover the blood and offal.

Gracchus climbed down the steps and joined Falco and other senators in the dignitaries' box.

"Senator Gracchus," Falco said with surprise. "We don't often see you enjoying the pleasures of the vulgar crowd."

"I don't pretend to be a man of the people,"

Gracchus said. "But I do try to be a man for the people."

The senators chuckled.

Colosseum impresario Cassius strode grandly onto the main arch overlooking the arena floor and surveyed the crowd. It was a full house, and they had already begun to chant the name of their hero. "Maximus . . . Maximus . . . Maximus . . ."

A door opened at one end of the oval and a dozen large mule-drawn wagons were driven into the arena. The wagons were covered with tarps, piquing the interest of the crowd. The wagons were positioned equidistant around the edges of the floor.

Cassius nodded to his master of music. Instantly drums rolled and pipes bellowed. Silence then fell. The audience watched in rapt attention.

"Now, people of Rome," Cassius boomed, "on the fourth day of antioch . . . we can celebrate the sixty-fourth day of the games . . . as proof of Caesar's continued benevolence and the bounty of the Empire . . . witness!"

At that moment servants pulled the tarps off the wagons. They were filled to heaping with loaves of bread. The servants began tossing the bread into the stands. Other servants appeared on the top tiers of the stadium and tossed loaves down. It was a veritable rain of bounty.

The crowd cheered loudly and grabbed for the bread.

Cassius took the opportunity of this comedic respite from his nonstop orating to gulp several quick cups of water.

With levity and adrenaline flowing through his people, Commodus chose this moment to enter. He moved directly and expectantly to the edge of the Imperial box.

The crowd cheered him and his weird, novel surprise. They loved it.

Commodus raised his arms, soaking up their adoration. Lucilla entered behind him.

The crowd tore into the bread, eating eagerly and yelling Commodus's name.

Below in the holding cells, Proximo stood with Maximus as he went about strapping on his armor. They heard a great cheer go up from the crowd.

"He knows all too well how to manipulate the crowd," Proximo said.

"Marcus Aurelius had a dream that was Rome, Proximo," Maximus said. "This is not it."

"Marcus Aurelius is dead, Maximus," Proximo reminded him. "We mortals are but shadows and dust . . . shadows and dust."

In the arena, the bread wagons withdrew and the crowd waited expectantly for the next treat.

"In his majestic charity," Cassius boomed again, "the Emperor has deigned this day to favor the people of Rome with a historical final match. Returning to the Colosseum today after five years in retirement . . . Caesar is pleased to bring you . . . *the only undefeated champion in Roman history*!"

The crowd was going mad. They loved nothing more than the startling and unexpected. And they loved whomever could give it to them.

"*The legendary Tigris of Gaul!*" Cassius shouted at the top of his lungs.

The crowd erupted in paroxysms of joy as Tigris burst into the arena in an ornate chariot.

Tigris was a fierce man in his forties, his brutal, scarred face and thickly muscled body a testament to his many years in the arena. He wore tiger-embossed polished silver armor over thick blackstrap leather girdings, and a polished silver tiger helmet off of which the noon-high sun reflected in bursts of brilliant light. He sped around the racetrack rim of the arena in his chariot, his arm raised in defiance. The crowd roared as they never had before.

FORTY-SIX

Tigris waited, standing in the center of the arena. He carried a terrifying battle-axe, its bladed end sharpened to a razor edge, its other end tapering down to a wicked pick. From his other arm extended a long broadsword, attached to his hand like a prosthetic sword arm.

The crowd was breathless with anticipation.

"And from the rocky promontories and martial bloodlines of fearsome Spain," Cassius bellowed from the great arch, "representing the training lyceum of Aelius Proximo . . . Caesar is pleased to give you . . . *the warrior Maximus!*"

The crowd cheered and chanted his name.

Maximus appeared from his gate. The crowd's hollers jumped up several decibels. The star gladiator carried nothing but a short sword and a round silver shield, and his head was bare, unprotected.

Maximus's fans had increased considerably in number and in fervor. Among the devotees for this fight were a group who usually avoided this bloody sport as too common and tedious: a band of soldiers. They were legionaries from the Germania campaign, with Valerius and Maximus's former manservant Cicero at their center.

They had come to see for themselves if it was true that their beloved general was really still alive. And when he got close enough for them to recognize beyond a doubt, they looked at one another—and exchanged exultant handclasps. They shouted excitedly to Maximus, but their voices simply blended in with all the other fans yelling his name.

Up in the Imperial box, Commodus also watched Maximus closely. "They embrace him like one of their own," he said.

"The mob is fickle, brother," Lucilla said. "He'll be forgotten in a month."

"No," Commodus said smugly. "Much sooner than that."

She looked at her brother, not quite understanding.

"It's been arranged," was all that Commodus replied.

On the field of combat, Maximus looked Tigris over. *Only one man with a sword and axe?* he thought. *Something's wrong. What am I missing?* He made sure to keep his eyes open all around him as he approached the renowned fighter.

Maximus stopped a few feet from the veteran battler. They locked eyes, saluted each other, and then Tigris turned to the Imperial box and raised his sword.

The crowd waited eagerly for the immortal words, but only Tigris spoke. *"Morituri te salutamus!"* the gigantic gladiator called out. "We who are about to die salute you."

Maximus did not turn to the Imperial box and did not salute. Instead, he bent down and picked up some sand, rubbing it in his palms.

Tigris lowered the face plate on his elaborate silver helmet. The visor completely covered his face, giving him an eerie, pale steel countenance, with slits only for his eyes and mouth.

The crowd whistled and cheered as Tigris instantly

attacked, spinning and slashing. Maximus blocked his blows and struck back.

The swordplay was very fast and virtually equal in its ferocity. They thrust and parried and hacked like lightning, constantly attacking and defending at once. The two gladiators seemed perfectly matched.

Maximus nonetheless attacked vehemently with the same inviolate confidence and belief he took into battle: He had age on his side, he was in maximum fighting shape, and he never lost, not ever. He would not be killed this day.

As he fought, Maximus became aware of a strange sound over the roar of the crowd, a low rumbling. He turned and circled, but couldn't place its origin. Then he felt something, an odd vibration in the ground.

Tigris lunged to attack, and as Maximus backed up a step to deflect the blow, a trapdoor exploded open in the sand behind him and an enormous, snarling Bengal tiger leapt out and sprang at him. The beast's giant claws raked his back as he rolled violently away, expecting the tiger to land on top of him. Maximus scrambled to his feet and braced himself—only to see that the tiger was restrained on long chains held tightly by three men near the wall. The chains were operated through a midway anchor loop on the arena floor, allowing Tigris's support team their own degree of safety.

Tigris took advantage of Maximus's momentary confusion and assaulted brutally with sword and axe, forcing him backward again with sheer, brute strength. Maximus just barely evaded the Bengal's claws and counterattacked, driving Tigris in a new direction. He circled, testing Tigris's defenses, and was about to attack again when a second trapdoor burst open next to him and another Bengal tiger charged up a ramp right at him.

Maximus rolled for a new position and fought on, as twice more hidden tigers sprung from the ground, attacking him.

Four ferocious tigers now marked the four corners of the battleground. Tigris attacked relentlessly. On the defensive—fighting off Tigris and evading the four snarling beasts—Maximus looked in vain for a weakness.

Then all four tigers were suddenly closer! The teams of controllers were letting the chains play out, bit by bit, gradually reducing the size of the battleground.

Whenever Tigris was near one of the tigers, the men in the corner pulled the snarling animal back slightly. Yet when Maximus was near a tiger, they let it out a bit more.

The crowd roared. Fair fight, be damned. It was drama—a great fighter stalked by death in its most beautifully deadly guise. They were on their feet, baying with bloodthirsty ecstasy.

Maximus and Tigris fought in swirling action until finally Maximus's superior quickness began to give him an infinitesimally small edge. He lunged forward under the honed blade of Tigris's swinging axe and slammed into him. They fell as a tiger swatted at Maximus's face. He jerked his head back, rolled, and leapt up—to stand over the winded Tigris, sword to his throat. Tigris gasped for breath, crushed, stunned by the abrupt turn of events.

But then Commodus's "arrangement" kicked in. One of Tigris's teams suddenly cheated, releasing a tiger. It sprang at Maximus, who barely had time to turn. He raised his shield as the tiger crashed into him. He fell back and thrust his sword up as he was slammed to the arena sand. The sword stabbed up through the tiger's shoulders. The beast slashed at him even as it died.

Tigris had the few seconds necessary to pull himself up, snatch up his battle-axe, and prepare to attack.

Maximus was still trapped under the heavy body of the dead tiger, doomed. Using strength called down from the Gods, he wrenched the shield out from under the seven-hundred-pound beast with all his might and flung it like a discus at Tigris. It sailed through the air and slammed into the big man's visor, snapping his head back and denting the visor just enough to momentarily blind him.

Tigris was forced to drop his battle-axe to try to pull up his dented visor, while blindly swinging his sword arm back and forth wildly.

Maximus, writhing partway from under the dead tiger, grabbed the dropped battle-axe and swung it down with all his force. Its pick end pierced Tigris's foot, pinning him to the arena floor. Maximus shot out from under the tiger, evading Tigris's wildly swinging sword arm, and slammed into the giant, knocking him flat.

Maximus snatched up the battle-axe and stood over Tigris. He raised the axe, ready to administer the coup de grâce. He looked to Commodus.

Among the roaring, rapturous crowd, all eyes turned to the Emperor. The roar dipped slightly as the multitude held its breath.

Commodus, his face working to conceal his fury, slowly stood and stepped to the edge of the Imperial box. He stared at Maximus, then raised his arm and gave the fatal thumbs-down.

Maximus raised the axe high over the fallen Tigris as if to kill him . . . but suddenly threw it down into the sand next to the man's head. Maximus had refused to dispatch the fallen gladiator.

"You fought with honor," he said to his defeated foe.

The crowd gasped in a great collective intake of breath. A hush settled over the seats, before an enormous roar built to an ear-splitting pitch.

None cheered louder than Cicero and his comrades.

The cheers cascaded around the Colosseum. It was a thunderous celebration of the act of mercy, and of the delicious act of defiance in the face of the Emperor.

The arena exploded in cheers. The chant of "Maximus—Maximus—Maximus" grew to deafening proportions.

Commodus simply turned and disappeared from the Imperial box.

In the arena, Maximus looked around, taking in the adulation of the crowd.

Senator Gracchus, the previously reluctant spectator in the luxury box, took a keen interest in the crowd's reaction as well.

FORTY-SEVEN

Maximus began walking toward the gladiators' tunnel leading out of the Colosseum. Suddenly the area in front of him was filled with praetorians, their hands on their swords, blocking his exit.

The crowd's tone changed sharply, now hurling horrified boos.

The praetorians surrounded Maximus and held their ground. Though he was unarmed, he coiled for the inevitable lethal attack.

Then the praetorians parted.

Commodus walked through them and approached the great fighter.

Maximus glared at him as the crowd watched this new development eagerly. The Emperor and the Gladiator, facing each other at last.

Maximus and Commodus stared at each other, just an arm's length away. The crowd could not hear what was said, but strained to observe this incredible confrontation.

"What am I going to do with you?" Commodus said. "You simply won't die."

Maximus did not respond.

"Once more I offer you my hand," Commodus said mildly. He held out his arm.

Maximus made no move to take it.

"Are we so different, you and I?" Commodus said,

his voice turning hard. "You take life when you have to, just as I do."

"I have one more life to take," Maximus said. "Then it is done."

"Then take it now," Commodus goaded him matter-of-factly.

There was a tense pause. Obvious trap though it was, Maximus had to stop himself from leaping into it. If he took so much as a step toward Commodus, the praetorians would slice him up like an overripe pear, bound by solemn oath to do so.

Maximus turned and started to walk away.

Commodus glanced at his praetorians. Then he spoke softly, still smiling, still playing the gracious Emperor to the crowd who could not hear his words. "They tell me your son squealed like a girl when they nailed him to the cross," he said.

Maximus stopped. Then he turned back.

The praetorians tensed, set to respond. Some of the men lowered their eyes in shame.

"And your wife moaned like a whore when they ravaged her again and again . . . and again," Commodus said evenly.

Maximus reeled with fury. He took in his breath. "The time for honoring yourself," he said in a low, ragged voice, "will soon be at an end." He turned and gave his back to the Emperor once more, and walked away.

The crowd went mad! They cheered the defiant gladiator, their champion. "Maximus! Maximus! Maximus!"

An equal number derided the Emperor—laughing and jeering, they mocked him by tossing food and trash to the arena's floor.

Commodus stood perfectly still, watching Maximus walk away. He forced an indulgent smile—on the surface gracefully accepting the decision. Internally, he was a surging roil of bilious hate.

In the senators' box, Gracchus watched with rising fascination. Did he actually just see the mob throwing food and trash at the Emperor? Laughing at him? These acts of incredible courage were hanging offenses! All of it inspired by one extraordinary, resolute man.

Even at the distance separating them across the arena, Lucilla could read Gracchus's mind. And inwardly, she beamed.

FORTY-EIGHT

Ry and by, shed of his armor and sword, Maximus
emerged from the grand arena onto the street. He
was heavily guarded by praetorians, who kept the
eager throng of admirers well back.

Cicero was trying desperately to push through the
cheering crowd to reach Maximus as he left the arena.
"General! General!" Cicero called out.

Maximus strode on, hearing nothing, seeing nothing.
Crowds still shouted out his name, "Maximus! Maximus!" Cicero ran around the front of the crowd so
that now he was ahead of his former commander.
"General!" he yelled once again.

Maximus spotted Cicero a little way ahead and recognized him. He directed his strides toward him,
thinking fast as he walked. He began to hold out his
hand to touch the outstretched hands of the many
admirers. The guards chose to allow it.

"Cicero," Maximus said, as the guards brushed the
manservant back just after his hand had connected
with Maximus's.

"Where are you camped?" Maximus said, straining
to yell above the crowd's din.

"Ostia!" Cicero shouted back. And then he was
swallowed up in the mob. He ran ahead and struggled
through the crowd again, slipping out next to Maximus

when he came abreast of him. They exchanged quick words.

"How long has the Legion been in Ostia?" Maximus said in a low rasp.

"All winter," Cicero replied.

"Who has command?"

"A fool from Rome."

"How are the men?"

"Getting fat. They're bored," Cicero said.

"How soon could they be ready to fight?" Maximus asked.

"For you, sir? Tomorrow," Cicero said proudly.

The praetorians pushed Cicero back into the crowd as the procession moved on. Maximus had no choice but to stride on down the street.

Cicero, however, had one more thing to say to Maximus. He ran ahead of the crowd once more in order to get in front of the procession. Again he pushed to the fore and sprinted across the street in front of the cavalcade.

Maximus saw him, and directed his path to pass close by.

This time Cicero was ready with a little bundle in his hand. He reached it out to Maximus as he neared. Maximus took the bundle even as the guards pushed toward them once again. Maximus embraced Cicero, seizing what he knew would be a last brief chance. He spoke low and fast: "Cicero! Listen carefully! You have to do something for me. Contact Lucilla, the Emperor's sister. Tell her I will meet her politician."

Cicero nodded and, before the praetorians got to him, he slipped away into the throng.

Maximus raised his head high and strode on down toward Proximo's compound. He looked down at what Cicero had put in his hand—it was a small leather pouch. He closed his fingers tightly around it and marched on.

As soon as he was alone in his cell at Proximo's School, Maximus withdrew the little leather pouch from his tunic and sat down on a window seat where he wouldn't be overseen. He loosened the drawstring on the pouch, and inside he found two little ancestor figurines that Cicero must have retrieved from his campaign table back at the Danube front.

The figurines Cicero saved for him were of his wife and his son.

Maximus held them reverently, moved, struggling with a storm of emotions.

"Do they hear you?" a voice suddenly asked.

Maximus came out of his meditation slowly and looked up. Juba was watching him.

"Who?" Maximus said.

"Your people," Juba said, "in the afterlife."

"Yes," Maximus said, gazing at the figurines.

Juba thought about it. "What do you say back to them?"

Maximus looked at his friend. "To my boy, to keep his heels down when riding his horse," he said. "To my wife . . . that's private."

Juba grinned.

FORTY-NINE

Every brazier was lit in the elegant throne room, as though to banish the night. For an Emperor afraid of the dark, this was a night as black and frightening as he'd ever known.

Stalking back and forth, clearly agitated, Commodus spoke to an audience of one: Senator Falco.

"An Emperor cannot rule if he is not loved!" he said. "And now they love Maximus for his mercy, so I can't just kill him or it makes me even more unmerciful! The whole thing's like some great, serpentine nightmare!"

"He is defying you," Falco replied. "And his every victory is an act of defiance. The mob sees it. The Senate sees it. Every day he lives, they grow bolder. This is more than just a passing fancy—this is the beginning of opposition. You must assassinate him."

"No! I will not make a martyr of him!" Commodus yelled back. He began to pace again. And after a few moments, when he turned back to Falco, he was calmer. "When I went to the Senate today," he said, "I purposely told them about using the grain reserves to pay for the games. And did you note what happened?"

"Nothing," Falco said.

"Exactly!" Commodus said. "Nothing! Not a single

word of protest. Even the insolent Senator Gracchus was as silent as a mouse. Why?"

Commodus stopped, and gazed out a window into the darkness that permeated the city he supposedly ruled.

"I have been told of a certain sea snake," Falco said, "which has a most unusual method of attracting its prey. It will lie on the bottom of the ocean as if it is wounded. Then its enemies will approach. And yet it will lie quite still. And then its enemies will take little bites of it. And yet it will remain quite still. And only when all of its enemies are exposed . . ."

He looked expectantly to Commodus.

"So we will lie still," Commodus said. "And let our enemies come to us for a nibble."

"Yes, Caesar," Falco said with a slight acquiescent bow.

"Have every senator followed," the Emperor said. "I want daily reports."

He looked out the window again. Over the houses in the distance he could see the rising walls of the Colosseum. Already in the main street far below, a banner carrying the heroic likeness of Maximus was being unfurled.

FIFTY

He had been Maximus's man-of-all-tasks. Cicero, as the first-class facilitator, finder and provider of hard-to-get necessities for the general in the army, was the right man to send on this particular job.

Knowing where to find Lucilla was the easy part—the Imperial Palace. But finding a place where he might get close enough to speak to her was much harder.

Cicero staked out the main commercial street running below the palace, and from there was able to see the comings and goings through the main gate. He learned from shopkeepers on the street who Lucilla's entourage was, and the times of day she had been seen returning from her royal errands.

For two days he haunted the street. On the third day, at the optimum hour when the streets were bustling, a large, grotesque mask of Commodus, followed by a caricature face of Maximus, appeared. A troupe of street actors invaded the busy street, blocking passage. They set about performing a mime that attracted the nervous pleasure of passers-by. A dwarf actor, dressed as the Emperor Commodus, was beaten and made to cry like a baby by an actor dressed as the heroic gladiator Maximus.

Cicero, traversing the street, was distracted by the

performance—until suddenly the actors scattered, melting into the crowd.

Black-caped praetorians approached, pushing through the crowded avenue, making a way for a litter that carried a royal personage.

Drifting into the street, Cicero saw through the folds of side curtains that it was Lucilla reclining inside. She was lost in thought, eyes down, oblivious to any of the vibrant street life she was passing.

Cicero was right on time. He waited for her, starting to move toward the litter as it drew nearer. She was unconscious of the crowd, the chair heavily guarded on all sides.

Also discreetly present were two men in ordinary dress keeping pace with the entourage. One was a busy individual—harvesting information with one blind eye and the habit of turning his head oddly to favor his good one, seen at the café where Gracchus, Gaius, and the other senators met. A member of Falco's secret police, he had been watching untrusted members of the Senate. Now he was attending to the Emperor's sister's doings.

Cicero pushed close to Lucilla's litter, only to have the praetorians beat him away. He pushed forward again, just a citizen eager to get a close look at royalty.

As the procession passed, Cicero called out, his hand reaching out like a beggar's: "My lady! I served your father at Vindobona!"

Lucilla half heard him, turning her head to his voice, not paying much attention.

The praetorians swatted Cicero off once more. He ran around to the other side of the procession.

"And I served General Maximus!" Cicero hissed when he got close enough to be sure she could hear his words.

That got through. Lucilla signaled for her entourage to stop, and they put her litter down. She then asked her servant for a coin.

Cicero approached, bowing humbly, hand outstretched. This time, the sneering praetorians let the beggar approach closer.

"I serve him still," Cicero informed Lucilla in a low tone.

Lucilla's face showed a flicker of shock. Then she gestured to the praetorians hovering around Cicero. "Step back," she said to them. She held out the coin to Cicereo. "For your loyalty, soldier."

Cicero knelt by the chair, took the coin, and kissed her hand. Locking on her eyes, he whispered, "The general sends word. He'll meet your politician." He bowed again, and backed away into the crowd.

Lucilla looked expressionlessly before her and beckoned for the entourage to move on.

FIFTY-ONE

Proximo's School was dark and quiet, the athletes relishing the time to sleep between bruising training sessions and the all-too-frequent arena matches.

The master trainer himself was up and about, and he appeared at Maximus's cell and led him for the first time to his own ornate quarters without explanation. In the doorway, Maximus came to a standstill.

Lucilla and Gracchus were there in the dimly lit, memorabilia-cluttered chamber, waiting for him. The two looked out of place: Lucilla in a dark purple cloak with a silk scarf veiling her face, which she now dropped; Gracchus in his stately white toga with the exalted purple border only the senatorial class was permitted to wear.

"Leave us," Lucilla said to Proximo.

Proximo threw a deferential bow to Lucilla and Gracchus, then left.

"Senator Gracchus," Lucilla said, presenting him to Maximus.

Gracchus inclined his head, studying Maximus carefully. "General," he said. "I hope my coming here today is evidence enough that you can trust me."

Maximus's look told him that he wasn't convinced of anything. "The Senate is with you?" he asked.

"The Senate?" Gracchus said. "Yes, I can speak for them."

"Can you buy my freedom and smuggle me out of Rome?" Maximus asked, straight to the point.

"To what end?" Gracchus said.

"Get me outside the walls of the city. Have fresh horses ready to take me to Ostia. My army is encamped there. By nightfall of the second day, I'll be back at the head of five thousand men."

Gracchus was appalled.

Lucilla was quicker to take in the implications of what Maximus had just said. "But all the Legions have new commanders," she said. "Loyal to Commodus."

"Let my men see me alive," Maximus said, "and then you'll see where their loyalties lie."

"This is madness," Gracchus asked. "No Roman army has entered the capital in a hundred years." They were asking him to accede to breaking one of the great unwritten laws of Roman political life: Leaders did not bring their Legions into Italy. They respected at least the pretense that power and authority in Rome belonged to the Senate and the people. All five Emperors preceding Commodus had respected the tradition unswervingly.

"Gracchus—" Lucilla said, impatient with what looked like political foot-dragging.

"I will not trade one dictatorship for another," Gracchus interrupted her. He knew neither the depth of Maximus's character nor of his intentions, and could only assume the worst.

"The time for half measures and talk is over," Maximus said curtly.

"So after your glorious coup you'll take your five thousand warriors and just . . . leave?" Gracchus said skeptically.

"I will leave," Maximus said. "The soldiers will stay for your protection, under the command of the Senate."

"Once all of Rome is yours," Gracchus said, "you would just give it back to the people?"

Maximus's steady penetrating stare was his answer.

"Tell me why," Gracchus said.

"Because that was the last wish of a dying man," Maximus said. Then he added, evenly and calmly, "I will kill Commodus. The fate of Rome I leave to you."

Gracchus looked at Lucilla. She gave him a slight nod.

"Marcus Aurelius trusted you," Gracchus said. "His daughter trusts you. So I will trust you."

Maximus gave a small bow of his head in acknowledgment.

"But we have very little time," Gracchus said. "Give me two days. I will muster what influence I have. And you . . ." He held out his hand to Maximus.

Maximus grasped it firmly.

". . . you stay alive," Gracchus said.

FIFTY-TWO

Warming up on the ramp with thrusts and feints of his sword, Maximus was armored and waiting, listening to the building roar of the crowd in the great arena beyond. The sound now meant something new to him—power. Power that he could wield. Power to avenge the murder of his wife and child. Power to finally carry out the bidding of a great man whose wishes had been subverted by his monstrous son.

The sound of the crowd was suddenly amplified as the doors burst open. The roar surged in with the bright light—"Maximus! Maximus!"

He stood and took hold of his sword, looking like a statuary god silhouetted in the shining sun. He ran up the ramp and stepped out of the shadow onto the glittering sand to an explosion of applause. *"Maximus! Maximus! Maximus!"*

Lucilla stood on the balcony of her bedchamber overlooking the city. She could hear the roar of the crowd from the Colosseum, the throbbing chant that pulsed over all the metropolis: *"Maximus! Maximus! Maximus!"* She knew he was out there fighting. And that he could perish tragically with one slip. And perishing, take with him her hopes and the hopes of many, including her dead father. Her face revealed her anguish.

*   *   *

In the central chamber of his grand house on the Palatine, Senator Gracchus listened to the sounds coming up from the city while he busied himself preparing a large sum of money.

A servant helped him pack the money in a large leather pouch as the same anthem that Lucilla heard echoed through his open windows. It was the distant yet unmistakable roar of the crowd in the Colosseum: "Maximus! Maximus!"

"He'll be waiting for you," Gracchus said to the servant, a beautiful, doe-eyed youth with a serious face. "Stand at the foot of the Colosseum. He'll find you."

He held the pouch out to the servant, and gave a brisk nod.

Gracchus's youthful servant made his way down the crowded street, unaware that he was being followed by one of Falco's secret police.

Ahead of him, Proximo sat in a street-side café, nearby the curious monument that was all that remained of a Colossus: one giant stone foot.

Proximo watched the passing scene. He seemed to be looking around aimlessly, taking in the comedy fair. In fact, he was on the alert for Gracchus's servant.

To his irritation, his line of sight to the Colossus's foot was blocked by an Egyptian street performer, who was juggling eggs for a few coins.

Finally, he saw Gracchus's servant walk up to the giant foot and stand there. Proximo relaxed, making no immediate move other than to sip at his drink, smiling at the antics of the juggler. Then, idly yawning, he checked out the street. He had lived too long in the scorpion ring of Rome not to know how to take precautions. A casual head turn, and his wariness was justified. He saw a man loitering in a way he did not like. It was Falco's one-eyed secret policeman.

Proximo glanced back toward the giant foot, his eyes now keener. He knew the agent who had followed Gracchus's servant down the street was there for one reason. It was a setup.

From the distant arena came the cry of the crowd: "Maximus! Maximus!" Gracchus's beautiful boy watched as the juggler caught all his eggs and moved on. He stood patiently by the giant foot with his bag of money, but no one approached him.

The table where Proximo had been sitting was now empty. The canny trainer of gladiators—former champion gladiator himself—had a powerful survival instinct. He knew when to vanish.

Lucilla, writing letters in her chamber, could not help listening to the sounds pulsing from the Colosseum: *"Maximus! Maximus!"* When abruptly the crowd fell silent, she put her quill down and walked straight to the window, where she stood, waiting in dread. Then up went a cheer, and the chant began again: *"Maximus! Maximus! Maximus!"*

Her face brightened. He was still alive, still victorious in battle.

FIFTY-THREE

Maximus was brought to Proximo's chamber by two guards just after sunset. He stormed into the room expectantly—impatient to act, eager to get the plan under way.

Proximo turned from the window and dismissed the guards. He looked at Maximus and shook his head. "I tried," he said. "It won't work. The Emperor knows too much. As for me, this has become too dangerous." He made a motion of dismissal.

"You'll be paid on my return," Maximus said. "I give you my word."

"Your word?" Proximo answered ironically. "What if you don't—'return'?" The slave master gave a nonchalant shrug, showing that he had to take a practical view of the matter.

"Do you remember what it was to have trust, Proximo?" Maximus said, his tolerance for the man's self-serving nature strained to the limit.

"Trust?" Proximo said. "Believing in somebody for no apparent reason?" He shook his head in amusement. "Who shall I trust?"

Maximus held Proximo with intense eyes, revealing to his trainer his absolute belief in himself. It was all he had. "I will kill Commodus," he said.

Proximo looked hard at Maximus, studying him.

Then he smiled. "Why would I want that?" Proximo said. "He makes me rich!"

But in spite of himself, Maximus's powerful conviction had shown Proximo the depth of the man's soul.

"I know you are a man of his word, General," he said. "I know you would die for honor, or for Rome, or the memory of your ancestors. I, on the other hand, am just an entertainer."

It was a lost cause, Proximo was saying. He turned and signaled to the guards waiting outside. "Take him away," he said.

Maximus's steady gaze pierced Proximo's eyes. "He killed the man who set you free," he said.

Proximo gazed back, giving nothing away. Then he motioned again for the guard to take him away.

Maximus's footsteps receded as the guard led him back to his cell.

Proximo stood alone at the door. The rudius, the ceremonial wooden sword given him by Marcus Aurelius, lay on a table. Proximo's hand reached out and touched it. He looked down longingly at the symbol of his freedom.

FIFTY-FOUR

The word of Falco's spy traveled quickly from Proximo to Gracchus, from Gracchus to the other senators, and then to Lucilla. Their conspiring was known, and their lives were suddenly hanging off a cliff's edge. Lucilla, not one to wilt in the face of threat, moved to pull them back from the abyss.

Returning immediately to the palace, she made directly for the lion's den—her brother's chamber. He knew something and may have suspected the rest, but how much he knew, she didn't know. Did he have any idea that the hated Maximus was at the center of a plot against his rule? Not likely, or the roof would have blown off the palace already.

Always before, she had been able to work her magic on Commodus, calming him down, dissolving his paranoid fears, defusing his rage. She offered a prayer to the Gods that she would not fail now, with everything at stake.

The door of his chamber opened as she reached it, and Senator Falco emerged followed by two men. They were the two gleaners, the harvesters of information in intrigue-riddled Rome—Falco's agents.

Falco bowed to Lucilla as she passed. She scanned his face but it revealed nothing to her.

She acknowledged his bow, and noted the men with

him. From their ordinary clothes and appearance, she intuited instantly who and what they were—spies who had just delivered more secrets. With a pounding heart, she went in to face her brother.

Commodus sat across the room on the edge of the bed contemplating a miniature model of the Colosseum.

Lucilla crossed the room toward him.

"Where have you been?" he said. "I sent for you."

"Brother, please," she answered, and sat on the bed beside him. He reached up and stroked her hair.

"What's troubling you?" Lucilla said.

"Does Gracchus have a new lover?" Commodus said, smiling.

"I don't know," Lucilla said uncomfortably.

"I thought you'd seen him," Commodus said. "For three nights now, he goes out and returns late. He thinks I don't know."

"Let him have his secrets," Lucilla said. "He can do nothing."

"He has no secrets," Commodus said firmly, his tone different now, colder. "Gracchus infects everyone like a putrid fever. For the health of Rome, the Senate must be bled." He smiled an icy smile as he pushed a tendril of hair back from her cheek. "And he will bleed too . . . very soon."

A flicker of anxiety crossed Lucilla's face.

As her brother's hand lingered on her cheek, caressing it, she turned to him, her eyes on his, and said, "But not tonight."

Commodus, taken by her closeness, the pleasure of her soft voice, heard there a message he wanted much to hear—one that pushed other concerns away. He began to relax just a little. "Do you remember what our father said once," he said. " 'Life is a dream, a frightful dream.' Do you remember that?"

"Yes," Lucilla said, lying back on the bed. "I remember."

He leaned toward her and touched her face very gently, feeling the contours of her cheekbones. "Do you think that's true?" Commodus said.

"I don't know," Lucilla said.

He ran the tips of his fingers sensually along her full lips. "I think it is," he said, "and I have only you to share it with. Open your mouth."

She parted her lips slightly. He ran one finger along her dazzling teeth. "You know I love you," Commodus said.

"And I love you," Lucilla said. She then saw how intensely he was gazing at her.

She quickly extricated herself from under his rapt stare and quickly left the palace.

FIFTY-FIVE

Maximus was lying on his bunk in the dark, clutching his figurines, knowing that to doze off was to risk being slain ignominiously in his sleep—not a way he wanted to go to meet his ancestors. Staring into the dark, he soon heard footsteps approaching the cell area. Commodus would strike soon, he was certain. Maybe this was the moment. He braced for danger.

Instead it was Proximo who appeared, and unlocked his cell door. Rather than calling Maximus out, he entered the cell himself and gestured to Juba, awakening from a deep sleep on his bunk. "Out!" he commanded the Numidian. "Get out now!"

Once Juba had stumbled out into the corridor, Proximo turned to Maximus with a faint knowing smile. "Congratulations, General," he said. "You've got very persuasive friends." He stepped aside.

Lucilla showed herself, moving swiftly into the cell. Proximo bowed and withdrew.

Maximus, rising from his bunk, was very surprised to see her. But before he could say anything, she started to speak rapidly, in a low voice. "My brother's going to arrest Gracchus," she whispered. "We dare not wait any longer. You must leave tonight. Proximo will come for you at midnight, and lead you to a gate.

Your servant, Cicero, will be waiting there with horses."

He was very moved. "You've done all this?" Maximus asked. "You risk too much."

"I have much to pay for," Lucilla said. She moved as if to leave.

"You have nothing to pay for," Maximus said. "You love your son. You're strong for him."

Tears alighted in her eyes. She turned away to hide them. "I am tired of being strong," she said. "My brother hates all the world—and you most of all."

"Because your father chose me."

"No," she said facing him stoically. "Because my father loved you . . . and because I loved you."

He drew her hands to his lips and kissed them tenderly. "A long time ago," he said.

"Was I so very different then?" she said.

He thought about that, then smiled. "You laughed more," he said.

Their eyes met, deep in their memories.

"I must go," she said.

"Yes," Maximus agreed.

Neither of them moved.

"I've felt alone all my life—except with you," she said. She turned to leave, but he held her, drawing her close, and they kissed deeply. It was their first kiss for many, many years, at rest there in each other's arms if only for this short moment.

They separated, stealing one last look. And then she went quickly back into the dark night.

FIFTY-SIX

Lucius was playing with a wooden sword in the lighted palace courtyard, sparring with his two grooms. The amused grooms, using feed bins as shields, allowed Lucius to overwhelm their defenses and "kill" them.

Commodus appeared and stood watching, smiling at the sight. He moved closer, and the attendants stopped playing and bowed low.

"Lucius," Commodus said, "isn't it late to be playing legionary?"

"I'm not a legionary," Lucius said.

Commodus took a wooden sword from one of the grooms and sparred with the boy. "Not a legionary?"

"I'm a gladiator!" Lucius said, lunging at him with his sword.

"A gladiator, eh?" Commodus said. "Gladiators only fight in the games. Wouldn't you rather be a great Roman warrior, like Julius Caesar?"

Lucius struck a pose with his sword raised high. "I'm Maximus, the savior of Rome," he said. Then he lowered his sword to fighting position and thrust it at his uncle.

Commodus parried the boy's play attack, but his body remained very still, and he could feel the bile rise in his throat at his nephew's words.

*   *   *

Lucilla walked rapidly into Lucius's bedroom. She looked around, and called out to the servants, "Where is Lucius?"

A lady-in-waiting came in from the adjoining chamber. "He's with the Emperor, my lady," she said.

Lucilla bolted from the room.

She ran down the palace hallways, moving fast, looking everywhere for the boy. She looked hurriedly into rooms as she passed their open doors. A servant appeared.

"Where's Lucius?" Lucilla asked desperately. "He's not in his room. Have you seen him?"

"No, my lady," the servant said.

Lucilla, fearing greatly, opened the door to her brother's bedroom.

Commodus sat at a table close to Lucius. An open scroll lay before them. "Sister, come join us," he said with a terrifying smile. "I've been reading to dear Lucius about the great Julius Caesar and his adventures in Egypt."

"The Queen killed herself with a snake!" Lucius said excitedly.

"And just wait until you hear what happened to some of our other ancestors!" Commodus said in a jovial, storytelling manner, taking the boy on his lap. "If you're very good, tomorrow night I'll tell you the story of Emperor Claudius." Commodus looked right into Lucilla's eyes. "He was betrayed. By those closest to him."

Lucilla felt as if she was going to vomit. She crossed the room and sat down trembling across from them.

Lucius, busy scanning the scroll, was oblivious to the tense, deadly undercurrents that crackled in the room.

Commodus gently stroked the boy's hair, his cold eyes never leaving Lucilla's face. "But the Emperor Claudius knew that they were up to something," Commodus went on, watching his sister's terror. "He knew they were busy little bees. And one night he sat down with one of them and he looked at her and he said: 'Tell me what you've been doing, busy little bee, or I shall strike down those dearest to you. You shall watch as I bathe in their blood.'"

Lucilla kept her eyes on her son, a tear running down her cheek, her pulse racing.

"And the Emperor was heartbroken," Commodus continued. "The little bee had wounded him more deeply than anyone else could ever have done. And what do you think happened then, Lucius?"

"I don't know, Uncle," Lucius said nervously, looking up from the scroll.

"The little bee told him everything," Commodus said.

Lucilla's heart twisted in torture.

FIFTY-SEVEN

At that late hour in the Colosseum quarter, all commercial activity had ceased, and quiet reigned the streets. It was the quiet that made the tramp of marching feet, echoing off the darkened buildings, so ominous. The guard at the gate of Proximo's compound, close to dozing on the balmy clear night, heard the marching feet faintly at first, at a great distance. But he snapped awake completely when he saw the first light of many torches come round a corner far off down the street, fast approaching in his direction.

Proximo was on the far side of the cluttered, shadowy room, lit only by a flickering lamp. He was rummaging through his heaped belongings and memorabilia, having flung some into an open travel chest. He was preparing to leave, and not in a leisurely manner.

He picked up the rudius, the ceremonial wooden sword. For a moment, as he stared longingly at it, the bronze plaque on it catching the lamplight. He threw the rudius into the chest.

He bent to gather up some garments. Then he froze, listening. He heard the tramping of approaching feet, and he knew unerringly what it meant. In Rome, there was only one classification of people who walked down the streets in unison in boots during the night. He knew at that instant how he was going to die.

The marching men grew closer, their torches brighter, as Proximo's gate guard watched for a moment longer. Then the man melted into the shadows inside the compound. He did not raise an alarm; he thought it would be pointless. Instead, he fled for his life.

The martial procession heading for Proximo's compound were helmeted, black-caped, black-armored praetorians. It was a unit of sixteen men, all with short swords, some with thrusting spears, others with bows and arrows. They carried curved, rounded shields as well, knowing that where they were going, they might well meet resistance. This time, they might actually face a stiff battle, instead of the cowering paralysis that so often greeted their midnight visits.

Proximo held a bunch of keys tightly in his hand as he crossed his compound in long strides, moving toward the cells. He had almost reached the bars on the far side when the praetorian unit came into view beyond the locked outer gates of the compound. They did a sharp military turn and formed up before the gates.

"Open up in the name of the Emperor!" the praetorian captain called out loudly, failing to see Promixo inside near the cell building.

For a moment Proximo paused, without turning to look at them. Then he headed on toward the cells.

FIFTY-EIGHT

Maximus was out of his bunk and standing at the cell door, listening even before the praetorian captain shouted. He had heard the marching feet too, and knew well their meaning.

He watched as Proximo appeared through the outer door, keys in hand. From behind the trainer came renewed shouts to open up the gates from the praetorian captain, accompanied by the raucous rattle of swords on the bars of the outer doors.

Maximus watched Proximo as he approached the bars. "Everything is ready," he said. And with a wry look, he added, "It seems you've won your freedom." He handed Maximus the keys through the bars.

"Proximo," Maximus said, taking the keys, "are you in danger of becoming a good man?"

Proximo reacted with a dour smile, then turned and walked back out the door.

Proximo walked back across the compound, in full view of the praetorians. He walked with his eyes ahead, not looking at the uniformed assassins, nor acknowledging their existence.

For a moment the praetorians could not believe it. The man walked unhurriedly, completely ignoring them, not scurrying in fear, which is what they had grown accustomed to seeing.

Their noses bent, the four front rank praetorians

began shouting and banging at the gates more loudly than ever. "The Emperor commands you to open the gates, Proximo!" the captain shouted.

"Do you want to die, old man?" the first lieutenant yelled. "Tonight all enemies of the Emperor must perish!"

Proximo walked serenely on, and turned up the stairway to his chamber.

"Smash the locks!" the praetorian captain said to his men, mad enough by the snub that he was ready to chew ground glass.

Inside the slaves' block, Maximus had his cell door open, and he and Juba were out.

Haken and the other gladiators were at their cell doors, waiting to be sprung too, eager for this unexpected chance.

The hard clanging of metal rang loudly in the night air as the praetorians hammered at the outer locks.

Gauging the time from the noise outside, Maximus handed the bunch of keys to Juba.

Juba took the keys, understanding. "Go!" he said.

"Strength and honor," Maximus said, briefly clasping the Numidian's arm. After shaking Haken's hand through the bars, Maximus turned and ran through the outside door.

FIFTY-NINE

The outer gates to Proximo's School flew open, and the praetorians poured into the compound two abreast and spread out, looking for prey.

Maximus raced for the back training yard of the compound where, off to one side, lay stairs and a tunnel.

Juba, Haken, and other gladiators burst out of the cell block and threw themselves between the retreating Maximus and the praetorians. It would have been a balanced and bloody fight that the gladiators might well have won—had they had any weapons. As it was, they were completely unarmed. But that didn't stop them. They attacked the praetorians with bare hands, fighting like enraged grizzlies.

Driven back, Haken endured terrible slashes from praetorian swords, but his bulk slowed the praetorian advance until Maximus had made it all the way across the compound.

Crossing the back training yard, Maximus pounded down the railed stairs, grabbed a lit flambeau from the wall and ran into the underground tunnel. There he found waiting for him his legionary's sword and his forged armor from the Felix Regiment.

Back at the cell block, Haken threw a praetorian infantryman bodily back into his mates, and was able to grab a sword and wedge himself in the mouth of the tunnel where he could not be moved, blocking any pursuit of Maximus.

Juba cracked a praetorian's skull and broke another one's arm with just his huge, hammer-like fists. He knocked a third praetorian unconscious with a vicious kick to the head. Then he took an angled blow to his own head from a stave and a thrust in the side from a sword. He fell bleeding and unconscious, and was left for dead in the central corridor.

In the training yard, the praetorian captain shouted up to a few of his archers, who had scaled to the roof of the compound. Within seconds—*Thunk! Thunk! Thunk! Thunk!*—Haken's great slab of a body was pierced from fairly close range above with four powerfully shot war arrows. They penetrated his torso front to back. He looked down at the missiles, almost disbelieving their presence, and then toppled over in the doorway like a lightning-struck tree. His massive body still blocked the narrow tunnel.

A contingent of praetorians bounded up the winding stairway to Proximo's chamber.

They burst through the door, swords poised, ready to hack the cornered animal from his lair. They found the old warrior sitting at his desk by the solitary light of the lamp, the rudius in his hand, his back to them.

Proximo knew his moment had come. "Dust and shadows," he said, mostly to himself. But perhaps also to Marcus Aurelius, who had given him back his life, for what it was worth. He did not turn to see death coming.

The praetorians swords struck without mercy. Proximo took three sword blows deep in the neck and back in quick succession. He died with the rudius hanging at his side, clutched tightly in his clenched hand, running red with his blood.

SIXTY

Maximus, garbed once more in the armor of the Felix Regiment and gripping the familiar bone handle of his legionary's sword, felt born anew. He raced down the stone tunnel leading out from under Proximo's School, hearing the fading sounds of the battle behind him.

Ahead was the faint gleam of moonlight. And steps leading upward.

Maximus climbed cautiously up the steps, dousing the flambeau torch on the ground before he reached the top. He emerged through a low archway onto a shaded mews of some kind, a tree-lined passageway between the walls of Proximo's compound and the high city walls.

The leafy mews appeared empty. Maximus stayed in deep shadow for a moment, looking about him, assessing the situation.

From the tunnel below came the sound of pursuing footsteps. The praetorians had broken through the gladiators and were fast approaching.

The high city walls loomed on one side of the dark and deserted passage. Faint moonlight lit the bare pillars and parapets of Proximo's compound on the other. There was nowhere to run.

Suddenly, Maximus heard a soft whinnying.

He swung his eyes toward the sound, then moved

cautiously out into the street, now seeing two horses near a tree in the moonlight, one with a rider sitting motionless, in the shadow of the great wall.

He moved noiselessly toward the standing horses, slowing down as he neared them. As he approached the silent shadowed rider, he could just make out the face in the moonlight—it was Cicero, no mistaking those familiar features.

But something felt wrong. Maximus took cover near some rocks and whistled.

Cicero turned. "Maximus!" he shouted. "No!"

As he shouted, his horse bolted, and he was ripped from the saddle by a rope around his neck and was left swinging from the tree overhead.

Maximus ran to him and grabbed him around the legs.

"I'm sorry," Cicero rasped.

From nowhere, a hiss rent through the air and half a dozen arrows smashed into Cicero's chest and body. He was dead within seconds.

"No!" Maximus screamed. Hearing footsteps pounding toward him, he stepped away, spinning around, drawing his sword.

Praetorians came at him from two directions. From overhead, archers trained newly notched arrows at him.

Maximus backed away, brandishing his sword. "Who would be entertained," he growled. "Who will be the first to die?"

Slowly and deliberately, the praetorians moved in on him.

Only one hope of escape remained. Maximus hurled himself forward.

A wall of shields held by a solid line of praetorians blocked his escape.

Wherever he turned, his way was barred by a sea of bronze, and the walls were closing in.

A voice called out, "Take him alive!" A dozen men were quickly upon him.

SIXTY-ONE

Commodus had the power to throw his net wide in wreaking vengeance. To him, it was simply hitting back against those who would steal his rightful legacy. He knew his history. Countless Emperors before him had had to strike back against plotters coveting their power. The faint of heart—the forebearing, forgiving ones—hadn't survived. As a blood-red sun rose over the city of Rome, Commodus hit back hard.

The street theater actors were again performing their masked mockery of Commodus when black-cloaked figures raced past on horseback and hurled fire-bombs in their midst. The actors were engulfed in flames. The very public nature of the reprisal was purposeful, meant to terrorize those who had been entertained by the spectacle.

At dawn, before even the servants were awake, Senator Gaius and his wife were killed in their bed, hacked to death by out-of-uniform praetorians who crashed through the courtyard window with their swords drawn.

A few minutes later, Gracchus was walking through his garden, calmly feeding his chickens, when a unit of praetorians burst in. Gracchus looked at them and sighed. He turned his back to calmly continue with his task, but the praetorians dragged him roughly away.

Seven other senators were murdered in their homes,

as were an untold number of private citizens who were reported to have belittled or otherwise demeaned the Emperor Marcus Aurelius Commodus Antoninus, Imperator.

It was a blood purge, meant to cut down all those associated with the plot, and those who had displeased the volatile despot in any other way.

Commodus stood at the balcony of his bedchamber, watching the sun rise over his magnificent city, as his body servant dressed him in superbly gilt golden armor.

It was the attire he wore when he wanted to feel like a god.

Falco ignored the strange stories he had heard about the Emperor, more concerned about defending the personally advantageous and stable status quo than fretting about the man's peccadillos.

Falco was admitted to the Emperor's bedchamber and went to Commodus's side by the balcony. "It's done," he said.

"Gracchus?" Commodus inquired.

"Yes."

"And the others?"

"All of them."

"Very good," Commodus said with a slight, satisfied smile.

One task remained in the housecleaning, and it was time to take care of it. Commodus dismissed Falco, and returned to his chamber, speaking seemingly to himself. "And what of my nephew?" he said. "And what of his mother? Should they share her lover's fate? Or should I be merciful? Commodus the Merciful."

He turned and showed his profile, still as a statue, golden and magnificent in the early morning sunlight.

Across the room Lucilla sat stiffly, clutching her dignity as her last and only resort against this ogre.

"Lucius will stay with me now," Commodus said, walking across the room toward her. "And if his mother so much as looks at me in a manner that displeases me, he will die. If she decides to be noble and takes her own life, he will die. And as for you"—he said as he stood over her, looking down at her—"you will provide me with an heir of pure blood, so that Commodus and his progeny will rule for a thousand years. That is your destiny. Am I not merciful after all?"

He smiled and stroked her hair. "Kiss me, sister," he said.

SIXTY-TWO

Fifty-five thousand Romans, the greatest crowd the Colosseum could hold, were gathered, waiting. They patiently fanned themselves against the heat and close quarters and quenched their thirst with wine. Word had gone out: Don't dare miss this one performance. Blood-red flower petals from the hands of a hundred servants around the top tier rained down in the arena.

Below in the interior passages of the great stadium, chains jangled along the floor accompanied by the clomp of thick military sandals. Shackled at the arms and feet, Maximus was marched along a series of corridors by a squad of praetorians.

Maximus was bruised and battered, but unbowed. Only death remained before him, he knew, and still the hope of a soldier's death kept his back straight and his head up.

They passed a cell holding fifty gladiators, Juba and Proximo's surviving fighters among them. As Juba saw Maximus approaching, wounded as he was, he stood in silent tribute. The other gladiators also rose in honor of the man who was one of them, the warrior who stood up to an Emperor.

The praetorians marched Maximus on down the passage to an open space, where a large cage stood beneath the arena floor. Tunnels led away in all directions. Slits of light fell from above into the dusty semi-darkness: and with the light came the sounds of the great crowd.

Waiting in front of the cage, amidst the ropes and pulleys of the Colosseum's underground machinery, was Quintus, Commander of the Guard—former Commander of Legionaries under Maximus. And with him was his troop of grim and silent praetorians. The guards handed over their prisoner to Quintus, who remained expressionless.

Quintus indicated in silence that his men were to take Maximus into the cage. When this was done, the praetorians backed away and Quintus entered himself, to check that the shackles were secure. Bending close to Maximus, Quintus murmured so that only he could hear: "I'm a soldier. I obey."

Footsteps approached.

Quintus resumed his stern posture and withdrew to stand at attention outside the locked door of the cage.

Down one of the tunnels came the Emperor Commodus with an escort of praetorians. With him as well was a team of servants carrying armor.

Commodus himself was garbed in his glorious white-gold Hercules armor, and he moved with the stride of a conqueror of worlds.

Commodus nodded to Quintus, waved his hand to the guards, and the cage was opened. The Emperor and his six-man military escort entered, with Quintus at the rear.

Maximus braced himself, expecting to die in the next instant.

Commodus walked up to him and smiled, nodding up at the roaring crowd above. "They call for you," he said. "The general who became a slave. The slave who became a gladiator. The gladiator who defied an Emperor."

He gestured to the servants carrying the armor to begin preparing Maximus for the arena.

"A striking tale," he said to Maximus. "And now the people want to know how the story ends."

A guard ensured that the pins holding Maximus's shackles were still secure, while the other guards stood with their swords drawn and ready.

"Only a famous death will do," Commodus continued, looking the hero up and down. "And what could be more glorious than to challenge the Emperor himself in the great arena?"

Maximus didn't believe what he was hearing. "You would fight me?" he said.

The Emperor's attendants moved in and began to fit Maximus with his shin guards, gauntlets, and other pieces of armor. They had his silvery-black Felix Regiment breastplate ready too, but were leaving it for last. Maximus watched all this with keen suspicion.

"Why not?" Commodus said. "Do you think I'm afraid?"

"I think you've been afraid all your life," Maximus answered, casting around in his mind all of the different ways this craven tyrant would rig their fight overwhelmingly in his favor, if indeed there was going to be one.

"Unlike Maximus the Invincible," Commodus said, sneering, "who knows no fear?"

Maximus looked at him with pure contempt. "I've known fear," he said. "When you took from me all I cared for in this world—since then, yes—I've been fearless."

"You still have your life to lose," Commodus pointed out.

Maximus looked at him levelly. "I knew a man once who said, 'Death smiles at us all. All a man can do is smile back.'"

"I wonder," Commodus said with his snide smirk, "did your friend smile at his own death?"

"You must know," Maximus replied. "He was your father."

Commodus went absolutely still. For a frozen moment, he stared at Maximus, and Maximus glared right back. Then a strange look passed over Commodus's face: a softer look, one that could almost have been remorse.

"You loved my father, I know," he said. "But so did I. That makes us brothers, doesn't it?" He reached out his arm as if for an embrace, drawing near to the general in a show of good grace.

Maximus suddenly staggered, gasping in shocked pain.

Commodus smiled at the great, invincible warrior. He had stabbed Maximus in the side—a deep, mortal wound with a blade so slender and sharp that the wound was nearly invisible, save for the beads of blood now begining to drop from it.

"Smile for me now, brother," Commodus said with a laughing mockery in his tone.

He yanked out the dagger.

Quintus just stared, fighting to conceal his horror.

"Strap on his armor," Commodus said curtly. "Conceal the wound."

Two praetorians held the wounded Maximus up as his breastplate was strapped in place. He was unchained, then a sword was thrust into his hand.

Commodus gave another sign. The servants scattered, backing out of the cage. A team of workers pulled out the corner posts, quickly disassembling the cage and removing it, leaving only the platform. A squad of fully armored praetorians joined both the Emperor and Maximus on the platform.

Ropes squealed and strained.

The roof split high above and light sheared down.

The din of the crowd filled the underground chamber as the roof sections parted and scarlet flower petals came floating down like snow in the bright air.

The platform rose like a giant elevator, lifting Commodus and Maximus toward the harsh arena light.

SIXTY-THREE

The Colosseum was packed. All fifty-five thousand seats were taken. Another ten thousand stood wherever they could, eager for the promised spectacle.

The sun-drenched sand was covered with rose petals.

The fanfare of hunting horns rang out—Hercules's call to battle.

All eyes darted to the center of the arena as it split open. Slowly an elevator rose from the depths. On the elevator, there was not a man as they expected, but a sleek, black *testudo*—the legion's famous turtle formation created with the great curved shields locked together above and on all sides.

As the platform reached ground level, the *testudo* suddenly opened like a giant flower. The shield-bearing soldiers scattered, leaving two men behind them on the platform.

A moment of shock silenced the crowd. Then they began to howl and stamp with excitement as they recognized that the figure in the resplendent gold armor was the Emperor.

And the man beside him, wearing the armor of the Legions, was the heroic Maximus.

Commodus stepped off the platform, taking his sword from Quintus. He turned slowly to all sides of the arena, his arms spread wide, offering himself silently, gloriously, to the crowd—the consumate performer taking his bows.

Maximus stood upright, surveying all around him defiantly, but it took all his strength just to keep his dignity and not pass out. He saw Lucilla and Lucius in the Imperial box, heavily guarded. He noted Gracchus in the senatorial box, a contingent of unfamiliar senators with him, also heavily guarded.

Juba and the other surviving gladiators pressed against the bars of their arena-side cage, staring at Maximus, awaiting the inevitable clash.

Trumpets sounded again, and Quintus signaled a hundred black-caped praetorians into the arena. They formed a wide ring around the two fighters, facing inward, holding their tall black shields in crisp formation.

Commodus drew his sword, and held it high for all to see as it glittered in the sun's rays.

Maximus slowly bent down and picked up a handful of earth in his customary way, signaling his readiness for battle, though he was still unarmed.

Quintus threw Maximus's sword on the ground near his feet.

Maximus stooped painfully and picked it up.

And the fight began.

At Commodus's first blow, Maximus staggered. The crowd gasped. At his second blow, Maximus fell. And the crowd groaned.

Commodus stepped back, making a show of giving his opponent a chance.

Maximus struggled to his feet, dizzy. He was bleeding out on the sand, the sun dancing off the dazzling armor of the Emperor, blurring his vision. He heard the sound of the crowd, now roaring, now far off. The faces of the multitude swam in and out of focus. He struggled to stay upright.

Juba stared through the bars of his cage. He saw a thin thread of blood running out from beneath Maximus's armor.

Lucilla, in agony, watched Maximus, who now seemed to be looking directly up toward her. Could he see her? Instinctively she reached out her hand, calling out his name.

Commodus struck again, almost balletic in his supreme confidence—and again Maximus faltered. Commodus raised his arms to the crowd, and this time he was rewarded with some cries of "Commodus! Commodus!" The crowd loved a winner.

Maximus reeled. The burning brightness of the sun filled his eyes. And suddenly, beyond all of this, he spotted sunshine on an old whitewashed adobe wall . . . seeing a heavy black-timbered gate in the wall . . . the gate now opening to a field beyond. . . .

He hurled himself forward, as if to get through that door. He caught Commodus by surprise, landing a blow.

The crowd reacted with a roar.

Commodus liked the renewed energy of Maximus—this made him look even better. Again he violently beat Maximus to the ground. The crowd noise fell, almost a murmur now.

As Maximus defended against a vicious blow of Commodus's sword and clawed unsteadily to his feet, only the sound of the two men could be heard in the vast arena, amplified by the natural acoustics of the giant bowl.

Lucilla stood tall and white-gowned.

Juba and the gladiators watched silently, all waiting for the end.

Another flash passed Maximus's eyes . . . a woman stood . . . blurred in an open black-timbered doorway in a white wall . . . beyond which stood a lane through a rippling wheat field and by a cypress tree . . . the sound of laughter rang out like music . . .

Commodus readied the killer blow, his sword poised high above Maximus's reeling head.

"Maximus!" a face in the crowd shouted out in the hush.

Commodus looked around, angry at the intrusion.

The crowd picked up the cry. "Maximus! Maximus! Maximus!"

Commodus turned back toward his opponent, enraged, and launched the massive blow that would finish this pesky general once and for all.

Only a reflexive move sparked by Maximus's warrior brain, honed after years of combat, brought his sword up in time to block Commodus's sword.

But even as he did, the chant echoing loudly now from terrace to terrace—*"Maximus! Maximus!"*— flowed into the wounded man, lending him new strength.

Maximus suddenly rose and attacked, driving Commodus back, forcing him across the arena.

The crowd cheered to near frenzy, back on its feet now.

Near the Imperial box, however, a fresh, strong Commodus ducked under Maximus's blade and drove a weakening Maximus back the other way. Again, the end looked to be seconds away.

Buoyed by the deafening cheers, Maximus somehow summoned a second store of strength and repelled Commodus by spinning in a complete circle and swiping Commodus's legs into the air. Maximus sliced powerfully into his opponent's golden breastplate as he fell to the ground.

But then the world spun and Maximus stumbled, swooning. Commodus was able to roll to his feet and counterattack, slashing into the back of Maximus's right leg.

As Commodus pursued him, vying for the coup de grâce, Maximus saw an opening and thrusted at it, catching Commodus on the upswing with a brutal swipe across the right arm. Commodus dropped his sword.

A huge cheer erupted.

Losing blood, too sluggish to pursue his quarry, Maximus staggered, his sword arm dropping with the weight of his weapon.

Commodus, now weaponless, looked to Quintus. "Quintus! Your sword!" Commodus yelled out.

But Quintus just stared through him.

Commodus turned wildly to the praetorians. "A sword! Give me a sword!"

Some started to draw their swords.

"Sheathe your swords!" Quintus shouted, a decisive order.

The praetorians obeyed, sheathing their swords.

Commodus looked around, suddenly frightened. He saw the great crowd, heard the name of his enemy on all sides.

"Maximus! Maximus! Maximus!" the crowd chanted. Senators shouted the name. Juba and the gladiators also joined in enthusiastically.

Lucilla stood in silence, holding her breath. Her universe teetered on its axis.

But Maximus, the man they all called for, was dying. He could hardly stand. He dropped his own sword. He appeared to be reaching out toward something . . . a flash of a sunlit wall . . . a wheat field . . . laughter.

Commodus saw him shudder and crumple to his knees. Swordless, he nonetheless stalked forward and stood over the great Maximus—and drew his dagger from his sleeve. Expecting no resistance from the dying man, Commodus raised the dagger to stab down in a final murderous blow.

Maximus saw the blade descending. He managed to grab Commodus's arm and pull him onto the ground, rolling. Summoning power from beyond, he turned the blade and slowly pushed it deep into Commodus's neck, seating it with a final mighty thrust.

A look of surprise—then a fleeting expression of vulnerability, and perhaps regret—washed over Commodus's face before he rolled over on the sand, dead.

Maximus slowly rose, took one step forward, and reached out one hand as if to steady himself.

Quintus took a step forward. "Maximus . . ."

"Quintus, free my men," Maximus barely rasped.

The crowd was absolutely silent.

Maximus saw his own hand on the black-timbered door, pushing it open . . . the sun-warmed wheat field, the winding lane past the cypress tree . . . walking away from him was a woman, and a child running . . . they looked back, his wife warmly smiling . . . the sound of the child's feet running away along the road echoed in his ears. . . .

Maximus fell to the sand.

A great gasp rose from the multitude, then all was utter silence.

Out of the hush, Lucilla, tall and white, crossed the arena to where Maximus lay. She knelt in the sand, and took him in her arms. She could see that there was nothing she could do to save him, but she wanted him to hear her before it was all over. She needed him to know.

"Maximus," Lucilla said softly.

Maximus's dying eyes flickered. "Lucius is safe?" he struggled to ask her.

"Yes."

"Our sons live."

Lucilla smiled. "Our sons live. And they are proud."

Lucilla kissed him, weeping, and whispered, "Go to them. You're home."

Maximus walked through the wheat field, letting the grain spikes trail through his fingers. . . . The lovely woman stopped, and turned. She called to the boy, who stopped running and looked back. He then started running back along the road, toward the man in the wheat field, toward his father, coming home at last.

Maximus died in Lucilla's arms, as she laid him down gently on the sand.

When she rose, the whole arena was watching her every move. She stood erect, and turned and spoke to the senators, only the occasional tremor betraying the emotions racking her soul. "Rome is free again," she said.

Gracchus and the senators attended to her words, to the force of her voice.

"Is Rome worth one good man's life?" she called out to them. "We believed it once. Make us believe again."

Lucilla stood over Maximus's body as Gracchus and the senators filed down into the arena.

"He was a soldier of Rome," Lucilla declared. "Honor him."

Quintus's voice rang out: "Free the prisoners!"

A hand turned a key, unlocking the cages where Juba and the other gladiators were held. Juba led the last of Proximo's gladiators out into the silent arena.

The praetorians fell back in instinctive respect.

Gracchus stood by the body. "Who will help me carry this man?"

A few voices from the stands broke the silence, calling Maximus's name. Then many voices joined in. It quickly grew into a deafening tribute.

The gladiators took up positions like a guard of honor around their fallen comrade, and picked him up on their shoulders. Silent and proud, following Senator Gracchus and the other senators in slow march, they bore Maximus out of the arena.

Lucilla stood long in place, watching them go, her mad brother lying dead on the bloody, petal-strewn sand behind her.

EPILOGUE

The games were over.

Their instigator was dead and little mourned.

The Colosseum lay empty, still in all of its grandeur as Juba walked across the sunbleached sand, still strewn with withered petals. He felt no oppression from the vast emptiness of a place meant for thousands. No, Juba, now dressed in his African jelab and soon on his way home, felt only the relief to be free of the sound of voices baying for human blood.

He still heard one voice in the giant arena, though— that of Maximus, the great fighter, asking about his home in Africa, talking about his own home in Spain. Maximus saying to him at the time of truth to have "Strength and honor."

Juba moved to the center of the arena and found the exact spot he was looking for: a small patch of blood on the sandy ground. He knelt there and scraped down into the soil, creating a little hollow. He took a small leather bag from his jelab and opened it. He drew out the small carved ancestor figurines of Maximus's wife and son.

He carefully buried the figurines there, in the spot where their loved one had died. He covered them over with the earth that carried their loved one's blood, so that they would have an easier time finding each other in the afterlife.

"Now we are free," he said aloud, looking around at the grand, deserted monument to depravity. "This place will become dust, but I will not forget you."

He smoothed the burial spot over and stood above it. "I will see you again," he said to his friend. He grinned the broad grin he had for Maximus in life, the one he would soon share with his own wife and daughters. "But not yet."

He walked slowly out of the arena, glancing back just once at the spot, as the wind swept crimson petals across the killing ground.